ON OBSERVER'S TRAIL

ON OBSERVER'S TRAIL

TRAIL

(SELECTED POEMS)

By Armin Boko

ISBN: 978-1-956736-82-3 (Paperback Edition)
ISBN: 978-1-956736-83-0 (Hardcover Edition)
ISBN: 978-1-956736-81-6 (E-book Edition)

Some characters and events in this book are fictitious. Any similarity to the real persons, living or dead, is coincidental and not intended by the author.

Book Ordering Information

Phone Number: 315 288-7939 ext. 1000 or 347-901-4920
Email: info@globalsummithouse.com
Global Summit House
www.globalsummithouse.com

Printed in the United State of America

Contents

INTRODUCTION

Once poets walked tall monuments erected to their name. Down to neglect, which begs a question, Whence the demise if not by having chosen the way of smoke to irrelevance. All about form and sounds, rather than to deal with people having to face apart from daily drama collateral damage inflicted by wars and degraded capitalist system's extreme money gone amok.

Men or iron ore no longer any difference, both mere commodities. Loyalty is for dogs. If this was not enough health scares shut down most parts an economy coughing even before. Civilization that took millennia to flourish down to no better than a train tearing down the mountain with a loco driver stoned and no brake. Make no mistake we may never recover and go the way of Nero's Rome, Byzantine and other empires before. Eaten by complacency worms and blinkered by Political Correctness. If only told what if anything is correct about PC make believe Fairyland indoctrination. PC has killed our sense of humour, wrong? Just try to crack an innocent joke and watch.

Free style here does no more than serve as a messenger's tool with substance ahead of style and word play. That is how it used to be. Social issues, and mind you all of us suckers, at the core here are for most part studiously avoided by modern poets, more at home in expanding abstract feel good notions stuck in nimbus clouds somewhere. And modern poems are not meant to make practical sense. S'truth! Seriously, just look it up. Now do you still wonder why people do not read poetry, and you cannot sell, even give away an anthology?

I can only hope readers find something of interest here. This from a lone observer worn out and disillusioned departing the literary scene, for all the good it does.

By the author, Joseph Tomasevic, a retired scientist resident at Lake Heights, South Coast of NSW, pen name Armin Boko, also:

The Monsoon Drifter
The Fortune Seekers
Sector Seven & of Ares and Men
Sketches and Reflections of 2012
The Bitter Harvest
The Borneo Desert
Poetry of a Common Man
ENCOUNTERS
THE UGLY NEW WORLD, just published.

Lake Heights, June 28, 2021

TRAIL I

Stormy ocean top loader washing machine,
Boat your one and only company.
Just the same driving over land mines,
Deserted by Lady Luck all alone in
uncaring wide World, get to know
the ugly pock-market Lady Solitude.

As countless names you do
Come across in the street
Face to face for a fleeting second only
Failing to recognize one that fits, meet
Your new companion Lady Loneliness.

Light fags for something to hold onto
A High Roller like sniff coke for a kick
Double scotch for a downer, forced only
to observe broken mosaic
with many shards missing.

Spend hard earned money
on a drug fix hangover
endangering health, the law next,
Alas, what more can be said bro,
But to call you a thoroughbred loser.

But when to the bone toiled you have
Achieved incremental progress maybe
Feeling of good karma taken over,
As you enter the gates of Nirvana.

SNIPPETS OF INSPIRATION

Airbus 320 gaining altitude
Doing simply fine
It is me out of control
Heart left behind
On the ground
Of Mljet my island
old homeland
Those who shared
My smile and bread
When will I see you again - - -

More stars than grains of sand
Why lotus eaters still convinced
You are the flavor of the Universe - - -

Sad truth remains
Sweet sound of no psalm
Gets near the feeling
Of heavy golden ducat
Rolling in one's palm - - -

Who consumed
The darkness and
Lit the horizon on fire
Fresh dew calls
On a rose bud
Let us celebrate - - -

In thermodynamics of life
The more you have
The less you are - - -
It is not what you have

But what you do
With what you have
That matters the most - - -

Sugar ant hero
He climbed
To the very top
Of the grass blade
Studiously
Scanned the horizon.
His own alone he saw
And no other
Kind around
Thumped his chest
And proclaimed boldly
We must be
The Masters of the Universe

NOT IN THE MOOD TO BE UNKIND

Li'lle Joel Mum's pearl
Had numbers at school,
Or so he said.
Asked to give one! "Nine" he shot back,
Followed by quick-fire "Ninety-nine."
Only to be caught out in truancy act,
"You lying little devil" Mum erupted,
Ready to go for the cane,
"I know where you've been." - - -
        Not in the mood to be unkind
        Just happen to speak my mind. - - -
Some of us being more perfect than others
I knew not of one
Perfect in every way,
Until this single Mum moved in.
"Every male's a scheming bastard."
This she solemnly declared.
"All after one thing."
Good Lord a male I presume
Sent down a blast of Antarctic air
That took her sexy lingerie frozen off the line
Para shooting it over the neighborhood. - - -
        Not in the mood to be unkind
        Just happen to speak my mind.
The best dream I had for a while
't was a plane load of Banksters
Marooned in Saharan sands for weeks.
I auctioneered a ten liters water can
Half full of hippo piss,
Till Head of Goldman-Sachs

Bid a cool Billion $US and derivatives on future sales.
No complains not as much as eye lid blink,
He perfectly understood
Market forces it is called. - - -
          Not in the mood to be unkind,
          Just happen to speak my mind.

SAY IT IS NOT TRUE

(Northern Bosnia 1993)

Waters seem to have ceased flowing,
In the river a bridge spanned once.
Dead calm the weather drowsing over
Fog bound fields bathing in icy silence.
Not a breath of fresh wind left about,
Wind died with everything else around.
In lifeless space charcoal rafters by
Grotesque indifference to remind you
This place once called home
Vanished from the map.

Is that all that lingers in memory?
It cannot be! Hey, you out there,
Anyone listening in, be a pal, a diversion.
Be a friend in hour of need,
Say it is not true. Repeat it
In Farsi, Sinhalese, Russian or Mandarin
In any dialect of your choice but Serbian.
Just shake the head: "It isn't so, it cannot be",
I will understand plucking out of my brains
Lyrics to that old love song to strum along.

Good Lord on Leave of Absence,
Fate that has been offside for years.
Calamities lined up in tandem with war.
Enough attrition to test and wear out the best,
Till in the end, last there left standing
Forced to choose:

shout blasphemous obscenities at Ares
Till hoarse in the throat.
Hum a love lament.
Or go stark raving mad?

SCOTLAND THE BRAVE

In Dun Nan Gall highlands
Clan fought next door clan,
All comers as well to display
Hairy chested fogged brains.

Like Spartans fighting Athenians
Persians, next Romans at the gate.
Here McLean fought Campbell.
For bad blood and freedom lost.

Weakened by insane divide and rule
How only could the invaders lose?
Bar empire riling up against another,
Like clan of old against another clan.

Horns locked in mortal combat
Right to the bitter retribution,
Hung and quartered the losers
Dispossessed at the end of a rope.

Wheels of history rolling on,
Lesson sadly learned none,
Ypres war gas Phosgene
claimed more brave Scots.

Bloodletting not done, in coffins
More still to come from Dunkirk
Albion having lost daylight next.
Loses on and on without end.

At desert sands of El Aleman

Albion won here at last, and still
Bayonets drove into innocent earth
With tin hats in garlands downcast.

In tune with kilted pipers fronting
sounding off sourly The Last Post.
A legion of young who bit the dust
Away from Highlands and for what!

Empire close to comatose in 2021.
Laung mirk nicht over at last,
Clouds broken blue sky is shining
White diagonals on Dun Nan Gall.

Ghosts of slaughtered Jacobites
strewn all around the moors of Collagen
begin murmuring, not in English, but
Ghaidling the noble language of Celts...

THE BLUE GRENADIER

Nestled along the Danube banks in the Panonian plain
Stands a chapel that has been there for centuries.
Facing the altar, a life size statue of St. Francis of Assisi.
Villagers tell me summer or winter adorned by a fresh garland.
Picked by whom? No one seems to know or have the answer.

Chores accomplished on time,
Life stock and the Master fed
Francesca orphaned house maid's
Off on the way to the chapel.

        In the shade of a giant chestnut tree
        She lets a dream run riot, - - - there (!),
        Gleaming Prince's golden chariot
        Is about to pull up alongside.

Strangers called, not one
Looked a Prince, till one day
To the sound of rolling drums
She observed troops
Marching all in step as one.

        Called to fight the Ottoman Turk.
        Ground shook as Empires' best
        In goose step parade inflicted
        Punishment on the macadam road.

Hussars rode trimmed mane stallions
Shiny coats rearing on hind legs.
Fusiliers in starched uniforms with
Brass buttons shiny as gold, - - - followed
At the rear by tall, heads held high Grenadiers.
Fran's heart threatened to jump,

        Yes, right there was Prince Charming,
        Tall, blue eyes, locks of golden hair

Meeting her glance smiling.
You guessed it right,
Wow (!), love at first sight.
Gap in ranks closed in by mates
Fran's feet left the ground to taste
The first kiss sweet enough; later
Listening to the angels sing
She found out what the nights are made for.
Alas, this could not last.
At the break of dawn
The Blue Grenadier bid her farewell
On the way to re-join the regiment.

"Promise you'll be back my Prince!
 Promise your love will never die!"
Prince she called him a lance corporal
Deserter bowled over by sweet love. - - -
A year gone, hush hush news first
Then the frontline troops returned.
Not half as many as there were before,
And the brass epaulets shone not at all.
In silence they trundled past.
Hussars on foot, Fusiliers out of step
Many without flintlocks.
As for Grenadiers, no sign of them.

"Have you there seen my Prince? Fran would ask.
Any news there from my Grenadier love?"
Silent, they would just stare here and there
At the ground tainted color red with blood. - - -
With child Fran would return again and again.
"Have you seen my Prince?"
She would call out loud to the statue of St.
Francis.
"Why do you hide the news?

Fearing she was possessed villagers
Forcefully took her baby girl away.
Thereafter losing her mind
She jumped off a bridge and drowned.
Ever since her ghost haunts this bridge
After the midnight hour.

START HISTORY ANEW

(In style of brothers Grimm)

Get me pen and paper
To start history anew.
Achilles and Hector
Up for second round
Troy not about to fall.

WW 1 and 2, why
No-one ever heard of
And cold war no more
Just snow balls
Chucked at close range.

De-industrialization
Never happened
The biggest con job
Of all time a fable
It never took place.

The mega rich
Who shipped in bulk
Hard won technology
To the East all innocent
Not declared traitors by

Proletarian mob
As forecast then
Forty years since,
Fully employed
In clover to old age.

THE BRINE

(IN MEMORY OF **R.L.** STEVENSON)

The Life on the Earth
Charles Darwin postulated
Originally all came out of the brine,
Including origins, yours and mine.
                      Hmm, where then . . . the tail, the fin and
                      the scale?

Proof upon a proof scientist maintain
Readily explained, maybe
One has got to accept that,
Except for one, - which fool, practical joker and
                      Larrikin dumped in all that salt. . . .

No matter it killed more sailors,
Made more widows than
Hitler and Genghis Khan
Romantics spin lyrics of brine benign,
Never mention tsunami or typhoon.

Include me amongst the dreamers,
For I cannot let the brine out of sight.
It wrecked once my boat,
Had me all but drowned, and guess what (?),
                      Punishments all forgot'.

For Poseidon's daughter of many moods is the Sea,
From trade winds' long gentle rollers
To rock-like menacing fog bound ice bergs
Or the raging foam fury of Force 12,
                      And anything in-between.

Give me my Lord the blue horizon, clear head and keep the riches.
Hand on the tiller. On the compass heading the eye. There,
Prancing like a gazelle my small yacht bobbing on the ocean.
Land left astern under full sail and a mariner Thy pilgrim free
Who could not think of another place he would rather be,
                    Other than return to the primordial brine.

TO MEMORY OF HELEN

When I see your smiling face and
feel that breath around my neck
all there still in memory banks fresh, -
*   where only was I then I ask myself?*

That forester upstart who took my place,
in playtime without end when each day
came gift-wrapped in starlight, -
*   overgrown child, where only was I then?*

As more years expired the news arrived
over the oceans and land boarders many,
you had passed away lonely and in agony, -
*   where only was I to make a difference? - - -*

Forced to swallow a bitter conclusion
Ye overgrown children dream is a dead thing.
Take it as vengeance from Lucifer,
*   dreams linger only in tired heads.*

ULURU MAGIC

Under blue cupola cathedral's dome
One marvels at the humpback whale model
Mighty Wandjina hands cut out of sandstone.
Invasive molecule no longer, I may even ask
'What chance's there of a private audience?'

Stokers of Sun about to clock off.
Shadows creep along dusty background, and
Magic experience seems confined to
Karma of persona inside you.
Until a radiant face invades the car space.

'Howyourgoin' sport, gotta Park ticket there?'
Alas, magic's gone hard-landing back in Australiana.
 Since whitey's kind transposed passion into dollars
Our dream this cannot be, sidelined we stare at the sun
Arms raised to catch cups-full of empty air.

THE WAVE 2

Swept off your feet by burning desire
Or home swept over by tsunami
One and the same it is believing it or not -
You have been bowled over by a wave.

To just about everything
That one can possibly see or perceive
Mathematicians will tell you
Extends wave function periodicity...

Granted, frequency, amplitude, the medium nature,
They all may vary a great deal, so when in doubt
Consult Fourier, Marconi, Euler or Heisenberg
To affirm wave is a 2xPixnxf function,
Just another wave.

STORY OF SOBER MINDED NED

(Vibes passed around camp log fire)

I

Driving on without spare tire
In midst of WA goldfields
To quote the Bushman's Bible
Must be the stupidest thing one can do.
After second tire slashed by quartzite
Outcrops sharp as daggers.
Desperate to stock up feeling a fool,
I searched from a coppice outlook
Overlooking the scrub.
Spotting what looked
Some distance away a car graveyard.

II

Towering over me a tattooed arm reached out.
"Uncle Ned", he growled sizing me up.
"It's what Aborigines call me around traps."
Clearly Ned was not the name
Given after birth, though
In these remote parts it matters
None nada niente and nix
What you decide to be called after prefix.
Why, there are good many white fellers around
Permanently half pissed called Smith Something.

III

"Good on you Uncle Ned,
Joe is mine", I returned,
"Any relation to Ned of Glenrowan?"
There are not many Neds about these days,
Meant more or less in innocent silly fun.
Gone for a while when Ned returned
With two cups of tea in hand:

"Nope, I wish 't was," I heard him say, me watching.
Angular frame holding a big man inside
Sure, to have worn HM uniform once,
Given away in the upright posture
Civilians seldom get half right.

IV

'Don't get too nosey!' stands here for cardinal rule,
Hence, I remained silent Ned doing the solos.
He took time before obliging:
"Hear a word of caution bro Joe,
Turn on that GP 5000 d'tector
Around here and the Helicopter mount'd
Gold Police will swoop down, have you
In twenty m'nutes flat by the short and curlies
Fined and prosecut'd fer toast."
"Much obliged for the info'
Thanks, a heap Ned!" beaten down I tried to
sound brave,
Ending in a rendition of a childish limerick:
There is gold in them thar hills
But not for me.
All the loot in the world
But none for me.
All the Sheilas in WA not one for me.
He returned for fresh cupper to be served
A matter of fact patently unimpressed:
"Make that no m'lk and two sugars."

V

New tires on order stuck for days
I had to make the best of it.
Next morning, I woke up
After dreaming up pudgy ghosts.
More than ghosts in fact
Daylight revealed spoors.
Some curly squiggly sliders and

Wallabies' paws gentle on the soil.
All over it men who left footprints
Size eighteen plus to pass for Big Foot.
Around and around the tent, though
I failed to see or hear just one of them.

VI

Spasms of heavy snoring though I heard
Coming from the open kitchen door
Letting me know Ned was bunked
Inside the mosquito net somewhere
When a commotion ensued and
Growled out obscenities I heard:
"Get off the bloody table!" Addressed at whom?
None the wiser till entering the kitchen.
Was it a giant carpet snake
Or a rock python, the largest reptile
I ever did see outside of zoo.
Ned: "Crawlies around I do not mind
They take care of the vermin
But bro, not in b'd or on the kitchen table,
A man has got to draw a line somewhere!"

VII

Them Blacks, I hinted, everything is open all night?
They are here bro Joe even when they are not here.
You cannot see the Blacks in a black night
Other than the whites of their eyes,
Or smell the smoky hides, and
Only a simpleton would put locks on
To have it busted. And another thing
I take no cash, charge if at all on the card
For ordered stock and services rendered.
No cash here on premises and no booze,
Not a drop, that is what it says in capital letters.
It is that s'mple and guess what, no need for locks.

33

VIII

Raid the fridge all they like.
Mind you we get on, friend and neighbors
It works out all right for most part.
Just no booze here, not a drop.
No booze and that is a final.
Often I do find roo tail tied to the gate post
Or choice goanna steak half cooked.
Occasional lubra pops up to see
That I am all right, and then again
They know all about the yellow stuff
Whilst not telling; to the true Natives
Before we came just yellow pebbles."

IX

Stuck around for another day to kill time
Gubbo from the suburb I went walkabout.
A tribal man if only for a day.
Get a feel of what is it like to range on foot
Without access to a gas pedal or aircon.
To be like a black man if only for a day,
Just me, GPO finder Garmin
Ten liters of water and empty tucker bag. - - -

X

Returning on dark, knee joints hot on friction.
Boots that failed to keep dirt outside blistering toes
inside.
Pants infested with spinifex spikes
Driving at your soft unprintable insides,
And backside on bull ants' fire
In tandem with clouds of flies
Hitching a ride driving you insane. - - -
No more! This ain't fair to a town whitey
One day will do fine WA, thanks.

XII

Before parting another cupper, I had

Double strength no m'lk and two sugars with
Tattooed ex SAS Neddy; a Digger who
Never was in love with Grammar
Nor she much with his parlance.
A man of principle far from sweet home
The soberest whitey North of Capricorn. - - -
XIII

Sun rose in the East temperature rising,
Guided by strewn beer bottles and cans.
No need for road maps.
In love with the 4x4 machine,
I hit the Northern Highway One,
Aircon on full blast to re-join my practical race.
Foot down on the gas pedal feeling sublime
Cold West End tinny in hand
Singing a happy little tune in key of #something
with none around to object, hi boyo (!)
we are back on the road again.

- - - NOT A CARING GOD, ARE YOU!

Custodian of the Cosmos
You let wind and waves wash away mountains,
  I If only the industrious twins
    Would wash away my pains
      To cleanse the soul so I can love
        And trust my fellow men again, but
          You are not a caring God, are you?
            All Life is sacred to be treated with respect
            In your image we are made
            it has been said, and
            I confess whilst killing harmless sugar ants,
            Never once did I question,
            Were they good ugly or bad,
            Yet here bold enough to plead
            Why will not Lord let us hear
            From the spirits of our dead?
Is it true in place called Heavens
  You my Lord grant reward
    For exemplary life of
      Sacrifices many and wants a few? If so
        Surely there is nothing we would love
        More than to pass back a word or two, - - -
          But you are not a caring God, are You!
            To super-sized ants on wheels
            The good the bad and the ugly,
            Decide please before more punishment
            Be directed and at whom.
            The good the bad or the ugly?

For in Your image and all
guilty we cannot be.
Pitted against omni powered,
But to beg for mercy remains,
Quantum Physics machines will not save us
This much is clear and certain.
Guidance's desperately needed.
But you are not a caring God, are You?

BACILLUS DESCRIMINATIS

Like Legionnaires' bacillus
The new disease
Thrives in air-con' blocks.

Air-conditioned
Offices breed the coli fast.
The way it is spreading

Farm sheep could be next.
Enter any office you like
Most classrooms as well,

And you will soon hear
The dreaded words, we have been
Di-scri-mi-na-ted.

By the Teach', by a
Colleague, by the Law, by what-ever
We have been cheated!

Our best's been cruelly denied
No telling what achievements and
Fame's been lost to the world! - - -

Mystified you ask
How settlers got Australia
Built in the first place?

FILES

"As if to breathe were living."/Alfred, Lord Tennyson/Odyssey

Fish can swim day and night
Never feel warm or free.
Man, can he really exist
Without Freedom's warmth.
A matter of degree to many,
As for the mega-rich,
They could not give a fig.

In Big Brother's domain
File-ISM dictates supreme.
From womb to crematorium.
Like a fish snared there is
No escape from secret files
Stored and locked in computer
Cloud monster banks storage.

On fertile soil trees are dying
Making room for skyscrapers
To hold more and more files
Built by men worked hard
Fed dry bread on a good day.
Busy engraving marble facades
Latin quotes for Caesar's glory.

Shackles and chain of old
No longer in vogue, replaced by
Globalization and Mega data files
To keep everyone in their place
And of this be dead certain
You will die long before
Big Brother deletes the file.

Centuries from now though
If History is to repeat itself
As it has been so far,
All this is bound to fizz out
As other Empires before
In ruins and chocking dust.
And just as richly deserved.

LADY GAGA

From Master Craftsman down to a bum
Not one or two breadwinners of by-gone age
But there unemployed Legions of good men

Meaningless stat's driftwood swept
On a torrent they join others
Like muck draining into Ocean of Misery

Out of sight becalmed in poverty irrelevance
Back-waters they cling to Lady Gaga
And me-me Facebook selfies for solace. - - -

Go away Globalization and 21st Century!
Go away Economists hiding there for cover!
Be gone and eat your own manured words!

(IN)HUMANITY IN GAZA

42

Child of Man struck down by incoming projectile
Fired from meters away, destined never to meet
Your executioner who fired the 120 mm howitzer.
Butchers of Guernica are back at work.

Blown into small pieces
Buried by avalanche of falling masonry
I hope little one you died quick and clean, unlike
Those buried alive in agony for days.

No tears of farewell, no voice recordings, no tombstone for
you,
No shame, no mercy, no guilt and not in my name!
Not in yours either most say, Humanity died with
Bulldozers leveling the forgiving earth.

BIG PHARMA

Clinch the teeth firmly
Tongue safely out of way
Numbing cold it is called
Eighty under zero Fahrenheit.

Keen on observation of Nature's ways
It occurred to me while idling away,
How only polar bear and walrus males
Manage to perform the assigned chores?

Antifreeze glycol for blood?
Some central heating unknown?
Naturally occurring stimulant that
Makes Viagra a harmless placebo?

I settle for the latest hunch.
Aye, it would make sense, and
You can suspect Big Pharma
Is flat out patenting right away.

AGNES DEI

He emerged out of the rain forest
Ancient pocket of Gondwanaland sassafras.
Like a botanical spirit he emerged
Silvery beard cascading down to the navel
Re-incarnated Druid from Celtic past
Face scarred by a long gash left by Roman blade.
Thus far, closest I have been to a prophet.

> It looked surreal with sunlight breaking
> Over green canopy into myriad of sunsets.
> Diminished all I could offer was:
> "Good day Sir." To which I heard a growl:
> "Another good day indeed granted to the ungrateful
> Underlings by The Master of all Life and all Things."

I looked at: His Ho Chi Minh sandals
Cut out of discarded tire.
At the sun bleached kilt he wore
Not for sale in any store.
At his left arm tattooed Dun Nan Gall.
He followed my eyes like an eagle,
Read my mind like an open book,
Before exploding:

> "Just wait for your turn at the abattoir stranger
> Already here in the Middle East.
> Orders and orders just follow orders
> Like Agnes Dei obedient sheep.
> **Screw the criminal orders, it is**
> About the only way Man can stay alive and free!

By the way you won't find any Aurum
around here."
Just showing off his Latin for gold.
Deflated ego I turned off the metal detector
And followed my new acquaintance's invitation.
We arrived at a clearing in the woods
A shelter of sorts, it may keep out a drop of rain
Or two but not much more.
After cups of green brew that
Shook me in my boots,
After a reefer of home grown that made me cough
I heard him say it first in guttural Ghaidling,
The noble language of Celts
Subsequently translated for me:
"Good by my friend, there is
Opus Dei, God's unfinished work to do."
I looked at a place where he just sat
And all I could see was green forest.

        When I woke up, I could not tell
        Was it a dream or for real
        And then I ask you
        In this world perverted beyond measure
        Where money buys Pollies, Banksters et al
        And you cannot believe a word they say, - - -
        Would it make a real difference?

A NOT SO HAPPY LIMERICK

All day lo-o-ong I could drive
This old bomb a car of mine
All day lo-o-ong, oh yeah
As happy as a man can be
And sing a happy little tune,
Until a sex bomb
Hawking wares
On the footpath
Got me undone, - - -

She ge-ets me undone and
Steers my little sedan into
The back of a-a-a
Leyland bus. - - -
Inside confessional
In time all shook up:

"My good Padre
One look at the damage,
It was all mine.
Bus with a big fat arse
Rear bumper bar
Of high tensile steel
Gauge sixteen
Had not a scratch,
How could I win (?) - - -

No contest at all Padre.
And then the chuckles
I heard from the foot path
To rub the salt in! - - -
Will this do for penance?"

SPIN MASTERS AT WORK

'Greed is good and inequalities desired.'
Good for 0.1% no doubt exceptionally good indeed.
> **Yeah, the rest can wait for crumbs to fall**
> **From rich man's table; bad for the 99.9 %.**
> **Now that is some (Pluto) not (demo) cracy!**
> **Also bad.**

'All men are brothers
And equal before the Law.'
> **Yeah, brothers like Able and Cain it seems.**
> **Equal like 10 QCs contesting a lonely solicitor.**
> **They could not be less equal. Also bad.**

'Never lay a hand on a spoiled brat!'
Demand the politically correct, bent on thought control.
'It may upset brat's delicate balance.' What nonsense!
> **As if he had one, just try**
> **Growing roses in a pigsty,**
> **Or cuddling to a viper.**

'It's a thriving democracy we live in!'
> **Really? Democracy died, we are Monetarism,**
> **As per Muppet Masters media moguls**
> **Who own everything pollies included.**
> **De-mo-cra-cy, a good name for a girl.**

'You can never fool all of the people all of the time.'
> **No need to, for what matters**
> **Get corrupt politicians to do it for you,**

Failed leaders and/or warmongers re-elected.

"Banks too big to fail." The critical call in 2008 made
    By Mr. Cannot Do President Obama,
    Masquerading as a man of Peace.
    Instead to put broke Banksters behind bars
    He bailed them out and left folks in the ditch.

'Israel has right to defend itself!'
Yeah, immune from War Crimes!
    Given God's right to bomb UN schools and
    shelters
    No doubt; and courtesy US taxpayer dollar to
    Steal other's land; build A bombs.
    Run apartheid behind tall walls then call it
    Peace loving democracy.
    What eye-wash and tripe?

'Factory hands in the West slacking
Ought to kowtow on Chinese wage!'
    So proclaims the CEO who get paid
    Hundreds of times what a Chinese Boss
    takes home.

'Economical rationalism', phew, try irrationalism
'Globalization's great', phew, you do not say.
'Level playing fields', three bags full Sir,
And myriad of other master pieces confetti; - - -

Just give us a break, spare us from
Any more nauseous catchy slogans
Flooding media to the dew point
With another batch of tripe left
Kept best for the next elections.

ALLONS ENFANTS DE LA PATRIE

(1914/2014)

Not one reached his twenty-first all NSW
Volunteers from Longreach and Young.
By fogged brains made to charge into
Barbed wire and wall of German lead.

Crowds gather a century later
In bountiful wheat fields to sing
Viva la belle France et Australie
Homage to the brave hearts.

Tricolor, Southern Cross on Union Jack
Hoisted at full mast flutter in the breeze
Watched over by patriots' soggy eyes
And Top Brass in sartorial splendor.

The Sun shines bright blue sky over
Polished brass medals, brass epaulets and
Brass band plays Marseillaise..
To audience of red poppy in the fields.
 Le jour de gloire est arrive

True, the Sun shone undisturbed
Recruits died here cursing Top Brass
In charge of the meat grinder, - - -
Worse still, an insult to long dead
how could they hear a damn thing!

Brass for Staff, Brass medals, Brass epaulets
Brass music Brass cartridges and Brass lanterns

As if anyone gave a fig that those who perished
Here a century ago, cared none for metal brass
and could never hear another damn thing.

THE MACHINES #2

Gismos we share
Roof overhead with and cannot
Contemplate parting!
        With some of them we are
        When you calmly consider
        Almost on first terms.
On another angle,
They also suffer from neglect
The poor PVC clad things.
        Also, on the plus side
        You must admit, they won't
        Cheat or abuse one.
Nor charge overtime,
Sick leave nonsense and other
Misdemeanor; so:
        Electrolux Freddy
        Lawn mower two-stroke Andy
Edge clipper Snapper,
And cartridge thirsty
Printer Francis, I wish you
Benign environs,
Conscientious Boss,
Timed maintenance and
Spare parts to last.

ATTILA THE HUN

Not a blade of grass
Grew where Attila the Hun
Rode with his horde.
    Only years later
    Composted by slain victims
    Steppe grass grew tall enough
Hiding from our view
Steppe's wild riders and their
Mongolian horse.

RECLUSE AT HOME

Under luxurious rain forest
Green canopy suspended by
Columns of huon pine trees
Inside au naturel cathedral
Rays of sunlight disperse
And pearly rain droplets
Cascade to the ground.

Enter wooden hut's
Single squeaky door
Of no fixed address
And no power lines
Where he combs despair
Born by modern commerce
Out of his hair.

Share the space he does
With whoop birds heard
But seldom seen and
Nocturnal native denizens
Shy no more having got'
Used to having him around.

For any place short of
Mod-cons can be a home
Without a parking lot
The Internet
Economical dogma
Fiscal ball and chains.

Place where one can
Come and go is a home

When free to call the
Four walls thatched over all your own.
Not Bank's breathing down your neck
Ready to call pre-empt default.- - -

Is not this how way back
Hardy forefathers survived
Living not in open sewer slums.
Sharing good air water and light
Until lemming like pestilence
They lost the clean environment, the plot
And multi-multi-multiplied.

THE GRANDPA

Whatever it was
He, model of my childhood
Only ever said it once,
Or not at all.
To express contempt
For trivial nonsense
Out of the corner of his mouth
He would send spittle flying precisely aimed
In artillery shell locus down to the ground.
Cherry wood pipe momentarily hand held.

> *None had fortitude to comment upon*
> *Le grand amour Tobacco's carcinome, or*
> *Grandpa contemplating aloud when*
> *Loading neurons into magazine*
> *Eyebrows stapled together straining*
> *Bushy moustache*
> *Tweaked for re-assurance.*

Ex Blue Grenadier with bear paws for hands
Made for hard work and welding rods
He would perform miracles on blacksmith's anvil
Shaping red hot iron with consummate ease
Shaping metal to his will as if it was baker's dough.

> *They had come from miles around*
> *For old Ziggy to fix repair the impossible.*
> *And if not, enough money they had*
> *He would send them back with goods repaired:*
> *"God bless you my errant son,*
> *This way or that a way, we all pays one day."-*

One Sunday they packed Grandpa
Inside a varnished timber box

To face our Maker pipe by his side,
Thirty years plus old greasy hat and war medals.
People attired black; many I had never seen before gathered
Under drizzling rain outside of graveyard chapel.
                    In fine eulogy Padre spoke of
                    A model of manhood.
                    How we will all be true to Lord Jesus
                    A lot poorer for him gone sadly to be missed;

                    - - -

                    And then to this day I recall a bell toll as
One by one they silently departed.
Grandchild orphan left there last
At his graveside's earth freshly disturbed.
Like Saint Sebastian shot up under arrows hail of
Anguish fear and pain.
A child cold wet to the bone.

BACK TO FRONT
(TNORF OT KCAB)

Where only is meaning to
Garrulous outpourings no end.
Ten bedroom mansion and no home.
Trillions on bank accounts
And people starving.
To a religion without a song, or
Snowflakes melting before they land.
How can it be (?) it is:

So quick to destroy,
A mere second enough to blow up a bridge,
So damn hard,
Years to build.
       So pleasant to fall pregnant,
       Probably unintended,
       So long to bear a child, predicted
       Delivery and pain hand in hand.
So easy to insult and wound
In rush of blood to the head,
So hard to heal and apologize
When cool heads prevail.
       So easy to spend
       Seduced by credit and glitter,
       So hard to save in self-denial
       And so bitter.
So easy to be a hawk
And start a bloody war,
So hard to be donor of peace
A healer and a dove.
       So many ways to see a man

Die in agony and screams,
Only one way to love him.
We could go on,
If this is not back to front then what?

If only one could reverse the order, so
It became hard to destroy and easy to build,
Wait! that's utopia, paradise you object,
Conversely what we have is man-made Hell
So much for vaunted human intelligence!

WIDOW'S LAST SON

/Northern Bosnia 1992/

On sunset platoon rode
Down from the hills.
Wide eyed wild men
Surrounded the farmstead
At the point of loaded gun
In her face they demanded
Moonshine, gold and money.
Spared none she gave them all,
Including the wedding ring,
Left none for her poor self,
Alas worse was to come.
Not content drunks hollering
For blood took him away.

       Lost to merciless war,
       Last one of her four sons
       But an innocent child
       Of thirteen young years.
       She went down on her knees
       Before the Serbian Captain,
       She begged for mercy,
       She begged for pity,
       She begged in vain.
       'Would you men do this
       To your own mother?'
       She pleaded; reply came
       None in words rather,
       Brutes just for fun,
       Shot up the place,

Then took him away.
Bound in wire
In fits of laughter
They mocked him,
Shaking from fear
About to wet the pants.
But an innocent boy
Of thirteen young years.
She pleaded and cried,
She cried bitterly, she cried
Till the night fell she cried,
'fore she saw a rifle fire
A bullet rang and there
The widow died brokenhearted.

TRAIL II

On this History class field excursion
    I met a man showing clearly
        Healed Roman crucifixion wounds.
"Shalom, you must be Jesus?" I called out.
      "Aye my pilgrim, just one of many,
        And who may you be?" enquired He.
Whereupon saddened beyond tears, 'because I thought He knew
      Colored blue I pushed onward
        Toward Mt. Sinai through clouds of chocking sand

Whipped up by Saharan wind Simoun.
      When I saw giant of a man long-haired and bearded
        Dressed in silvery robe
Walking on air towards me.
      I did boldly ask: "Sire, you sure as peppers must be Moses?"
        "Aye", he growled back mightily upset:
"You thieves, **gimme** back my Ten Commandments!"
      Feeling made Lucifer's apprentice, chastised thus,
        Guilty and all joints aching I continued

On foot journey through more Saharan hot sands.
      Fossilized caterpillar tracks I walked upon, and
        Watched buried WW2 soldiers dust off
After years and years coming back to life reaching for their tin hats.
      Them I did comfort: "Glory to brave hearts!
        Ye men died here so we can be free, right?"
          Whence as one they began to violently gyrate
Shouting back international obscenities at me:
      "Bollocks, Scheisse and Merde (!) Mister, Herr and Signore
        It is a white lie; there is no glory in bloody war!

Put back in my place once more, catapulted next
        I made it across the Giant Sea into land where

False Messiahs ride metallic birds and dollar sign precedes everything,
        Jesus and Moses having disappeared from rear vision view.
                In their place amorphous mass of mute bipedal I saw

Factories manned where insect like,
        Slave-driven by Golden Calf to imitate robots 24/7
                They all move one like the other
In rhythm of clocks ticking away madly.
        In tune with redundancy whips cracking overhead.
                In numbing repetitious drudgery.

And all this for bits of papyrus they call money.
        Worst invention of all time by far, for
                Ever since this lot's been off their heads
Demanding more and more there be,
        Louder and louder
                More, more mouths call to feed from empty seas.
Sadly, with no-one left in Carpenter Joseph's household
        Able to feed the hungry masses
                On a loaf of bread and a few sardines.

LOST FRIEND

Wintry nights are long and cold
My old friend let it be said.
Longer and colder since you have gone.
And still of your there is scent in the air,
I see images of rearranged furniture,
And scattered notes
In the room where once you have created.

Long walks through forest
We had outside of time
Passionately discussing
Psychosis of this world,
Evils on grand scale
And petty point scoring
For no good purpose.
It was all there no denying.
Despite all this with you gone
There is less left of mine.

Never parsimonious with words
Sharp tongues fenced for touché
As if there was still much noble
Worth spilling blood for fickle breed
Spoiled and perverted beyond measure. - - -
So here I stand my friend to have it un-said.

WARM TEARS AND RED GUMS DYING

Visit Wilcannia township in Western NSW
On the banks of River Darling ready to experience
Heartburn, washed over by
Warm tears after a long drought.

Darling River no longer a darling.
No more flow and red gums dyeing.

Here driven to despair Teachers
Bribe children with silly games.
Come and go as you please. It is a
Hopeless task to keep them in class.

Imps scamper out of sight
Upon Algebras first hint.
Gone walkabout day-dreaming
Footy stardom along the track.

Night falls upon a feral gang.
Ten year-olds gather about to raid
Farmsteads having tested steelwork of
The grocery shop last one in town.

Inside air-con rooms
Pollies present papers based
Upon imaginary advances
Backed by dodgy statistics,

While along dusty outback tracks

Strewn junk and empty plonk bottles
Police have given up, Law is an ass
And the clocks run anti-clockwise.

Oh, him Darling River, no longer a darling,
No more flow and red gums dyeing.

28-AUGUST 2019

FOR MILLIE

Oncologists s one set firm on
Six months at the most and
She took the news bravely
Despite breaking up inside. - - -
After a long, long pause she looked not at him
But through him with courage he will never have
Suggesting: *"Make that twelve my friend!*
Burn the candle at each end!
It counts for double and forgo therapy
That makes the hair go."

In between few good moments
She would play Chopin's Nocturne in A
Or Schumann's Etude.
Times of sublime musical chords
For precious little time it did last.
Moved next to a Palliative Care ward
Lit by a diffuse beam of light
That strayed in from the Pacific Ocean
Millie would have him comb
long brunette hair reading poems.

- - - And six months 't was to the end and not twelve.
At the break of another cold dawn
She slipped away without a sound
Icy cold hands still clutching his. - - -
Years later volumes of Tennyson and Nazor
Remain unopened and dust gathers
On old Petroff out of tune from non-use.
Her room remained unattended,
And he cannot stand to listen
To Etudes or a Nocturne
Without walking out of the room.

SOMBER THOUGHTS

Crystal chandeliers cannot make a fellow
Embrace a beam of light as
Surfacing from a coal mine can.

Nor can one after binge ever appreciate
How sweet a drop of water can taste.
Ask one hallucinating in desert sands.

Or how could a celeb possibly have a clue
What difference a kind word can make?
Just visit one languishing bed-ridden! - - -

Oh, "Life is short and then
You're a long time dead",
A friend of mine said,
And he ain't yet dead
So how would he know?

But dead a fellow must be
Never to come back,
Mortus and defenseless,
Stone clinically dead,
Dead as dead can be

When nieces and nephews
He never knew he had
Swoop in exultations
Of the wonderful Uncle
Testament about to be read.

WATERY UNDERWORLD

Vanguard ocean denizens
Advanced towards the intruder me
As into the brine I ventured weaponless.
   Amongst giant stag horn corals, clams and sea stars
   Beaver Reef ocean drop off I dived into had
   What from distance resembled my friend's
   Polka dots swimming costume attached to a fish tail.
Diving closer in it struck me as rather odd how
She managed to breathe in watery underworld
Exhaling no bubbles, but I need not have worried about
   MV Portabuoy crew's pet cod named Ulysses
   Darting in and out of the coral clumps
   Positioned broadside shielding the fry
   Between the intruder and its brood.
In age custom of good will
I turned empty hands towards him
Now look here big fish (!): no weapons to do you harm.
   Respond he did in a way that
   Took me off guard
   Swimming on course head on towards me
   Pictorial fins in ¾ rhythm waltz.
I felt ripples in my face and clearly heard sounds
Loud guttural messages of sorts.
How do you do, or who are you (?),
   Most likely one or the other
   In Cod-esque vernacular of course; - - -
   With big eyes the fish can wink
   And communicate, or what do you think?
Possibly asking: who in breath-taking
Villainy of human arrogance can claim
Other life forms on Earth to be but protein!
   Other fishes fearlessly swam

Towards me large and small,
And so many new friends I made in a single day
At odds with the world, I knew. Only to hear,
A fishing trawler one night
Had my new friends and Ulysses
Packed off to market in boxes on dry ice.

CLICHÉS PEOPLE COME UP WITH

Awash with **make believe**
Catch-cries, slogans **wrapped** in metaphor
Let us **road** test to find
How many if any **hold water:**

I hear: **'You're as old as you feel'**;
Why, only this morning it cannot be
I felt perky seventeen.
On cloud nine, oh what an illusion... **Zero next on:**

Tranquilizing dispensation to the poor:
'Money cannot buy you happiness.'
Add for double strength doze:
'All the best things in life are free.' Like misery...

Or why (?) 'All the good things are three';
After Guy Fawkes
Hung drawn and quartered. Yuck....
On **a less objectionable note,** though:

My Padre, the Bible you know has,
'Men all brothers, Amen'.
Methinks brothers more like Abel and Cain...
Then **fail not to mention** righteous ones who:

Straight faced maintain: **'Men are all equal.'**
Yep, equal like Dracula and Beethoven.
More like a **self-indulging** modern fable...
Next try is a **big call:**

'We live in a Democracy'; to dispel doubts
Propelled with media **plutocracy horse power**
And marketed by **best Pollies money can buy...**
Deeper **offside** still is a Yankee **fabrication:**

'Time is money';
No way Jose, it refers to production line.
If time were money, there'd be no damn poor...
Now Just **hold your breath** I see **height of folly:**

'All men are bastards!'
Glossing over the fact I must digress
Some do run up with wedding dress...
Just two more **pearls of wisdom** please:

'It's darkest before dawn',
Nope once more, look outside, were
Short of star- and Moon-light,
Darkness thick as soup descends at midnight....

Left best for last:
'We're all equal before the Law.'
So much **bull dust.**
A sick worn out worst of jokes...

Before I reach for more slogans skewed
On the head by **cadres politically correct,**
Femme-Nazis and cousins' lazy thinkers,
Let me state clearly how I see it all **mesh in:**

De-mo-cra-cy may well be like Electra
A lovely Hellenic name for a girl?
Money in $100 bills **Banksters** roll up to light

Fat Cuban cigars fronting masses eating swill.

Short of QCs, aye, **Law is an a**ss; but
Men ARE all equal dead, i.e., equally dead.
I also **bet my bottom dollar** there would be as many women as
men
Proper thick skinned scheming hard bastards all of them.

And rightly do they say: **'What goes around comes around.'**
Take Bacillus Gonorrhea. Yet, **'Where there is Life there is
Hope.'**...
Conclude the **sermon** with Daoism: **Go with the flow,** because
Gentle does it you folks and **'Happine**ss **comes in small parcels.'**

KEEP ON TEXTIN'

Spend before you earn oh boy
Do not be shy buy and buy
Latest must have gismo tablet
Before it ditto becomes obsolete
Called for by marketing aids
Your Credit Card seductress.

Determined to become android
Think you must in binary code
Paint without color and paint
Smoke but a virtual cigarette
Caress with screen images only
Find solace in gigabyte memory

Frenetic social engineering
Demands you comply with
Wiles of fickle economy
So, keep on textin' ye bloggers
Yo gabba gabba and the same
4 your Internet provider who

Loves ye all madly

& I xxxx U2

DREAMS I HAVE

I dream a world
Under clearest of azure sky.
I dream of weapons
Cast into tools.
Of New World rid of
Chattels, Lords and Majesties.
I dream Nirvana state of mind
Where truth is spoken
And many do listen.
Where one is esteemed
On purity of intensions
And sincerity of smile
And there is no acreage.

A place where villains
Ashamed redeem
Foul deeds
Of their own volition,
And men and women
Do not hide but
Hail their difference
Pretending inanely
No longer
To be cast
From the same clay.

We all know
It is free and naïve.
Dreams for miracle
That may never be.

Though' just to let
You folks know, like
Canine friend of mine
Trying hard
To make of speech
Some headway.
We will never give up the dream.

HEADACHE ON OFFER

When a metaphor contained
Within an allegory you find
Upended careened and scrambled,
Matured in dark a 'la Fromage, why
Wait long suffering reader
Could this be a modern poem?
And if the Headache
You do not see this a way,
Attend a Court session.

Villains on parade whispering humbly
There regulation dressed clean for once
Perform like stars in Actors Academy.
Devil's Advocates by their side pleading:
    "No, not your Warship 't was,
      The Alcohol that pulled the trigger."

Still of migraine no hint, hey,
Il *caro compagnero?* Sure?
Just wait to hear Economists expand
Why sums nebulous do not add up.
By then you surely will be reaching
For Headache pills double strength.

How so? Look back as far as you can
When has so much insulting drivel
In modern times of mass communication
Been dispensed to so many folks
By a manipulative crafty few? - - -
Hocus pocus and no rabbit and no hat.

(Humblest of apologies to RWC.)

MIRROR IMAGE OF SELF

I know you are there
When to most I do you say nay

When disconsolate from your eyes
I cannot hide

Like sun making shadows
Like cloud above rain

Like an optical isomer
Mirror image of me

Omni-present pursuing me to
Tanami Desert and deep blue sea

I suspect you are here
Even when elsewhere

Loyalty not your virtue
Ready to pounce

If there is a consolation
They will bury us together

Or can you alone rise
To torment another

SKULL AND CROSSBONES

Sling shot to cross bow
Claymore to buzdovan
Mustard gas to H bomb
Generals call that progress.

Centuries apart from Troy to Waterloo,
Stalingrad to sands of the Middle East.
Vukovar to Ukraine it has all been wasted.
Clueless we'd better go back to Aristotle.

Oceans filled with tears,
Blood smeared marble mausoleums
Under skull and cross bones emblem
Cave man is rampaging again.

Neanderthal's gone from Earth (?)
Who then are the Savages
Doing PhD on WMD
Killing Machines?

Fill the ocean with tears
Fill mausoleums with red poppy and burning candles
Fill the air with cries of victims burned alive.
None of this to bring back a single victim in the interim.

Skull and cross bones for new Zodiac, Brutus Savage PhD
Under Half Moon, Stars & Stripes, Tricolors
Or whichever banner works hard, harder than ever
Fingering his beloved offspring the killing machines.

FROM HAWAIIKI TO AOTEAROA

Frigate birds patrolled azure sky long before the F18.
Come sunset tropical beach would seethe charged
Exuberance of feet stomping as if on hot coals.

Lustful Apollo groped there after Eve's gyrating hips
To the beat of Native drums, way, way back in Hawaiiki.
Charged Erotica potent enough to seduce an Archangel.

White surf pounds coral reef since beginning of time.
It pounds sandy shore at the foot of palm trees grove
To the frangipani scent borne on the wings of trade wind.

Guahan Melville, Conrad and Brando
Interlopers all and many more landed here.
And what did they present to South Pacific!

Skyscrapers, motorcars and aero planes they brought.
Rats sugar cane war ships VD booze tourists and commerce,
Though in hearts of Native men old Hawaiiki lingered on.

White surf still pounds sandy shores if oceans rising
Ticking nowadays a monetary clock that makes
Legends of ancient Hawaiiki yield to TV Kai Time.

Frigate birds, they got lazy, vanished from the sky,
On the ground with ibises raiding cannery offal outflow.
Hibiscus and frangipani new hybrids smell of grass.

Leis recycled, watch Pakehas invited to a war dance
Laugh or cry, observe Ratu Francetich doing kamate.
See you at Hilton tonight, fifty bucks to get in.

Economy savvy mighty warrior race is doing fine
War canoes for museums war clubs for souvenirs.
In time of peace everyone is piling on weight.

Lazy muscles gave way to flabby lard; Kia Ora Kai Time, - - -
And white surf relentlessly pounds sandy shores
Under foot of a coconut grove as always before.

But is it Hawaiiki? No Sir, absolutely not.
From Hawaiiki to TEAROA or New Zealand

And then what with more oceans rising?

CONSUME NO MORE

Consume to keep the economy going
And help filthy rich get filthier
Consume to keep men slaving on
In factories belching foul smog
Consume till there is
Consume no more because,
There is no more left to consume,
You cannot eat money
And Saints only reside in blue sky.

Left standing room only inside of
The last breath of air fit to breathe
The last drop of water fit to drink
Sure, to be fought over
In frenzy by crazed mob
Free for all no prisoners taken
Last one's address reads:
    C/O Cave Manager
    Planet Earth

THE OBOE

In Memory of the great
Claudio Abbado (C.A.)

Oboe's adagio
Mournful vibrato
Makes me see
That lonely child
Trudge to school
Through deep snow
In shoes that carried
A big O
And my name.

> Timber reeds sweet talk
> Designed to console
> The numbed poor
> In their wretched place or
> Jilted lover's lament
> Fact remains
> Under Maestro C.A.
> A note was more
> Then just a mere note
> And a lot more still
> When played by oboe solo.

WITHOUT ME /CIRCA 1992/

You started a tiff
With neighbors
Since their cat
Did on bed of daisies
You know what.
Now go on warring
Without me.

You hop from
Bed to bed
Then come back
With "I love you."
No more bed-hopping,
One bed should do.
Go on
Without me
See if I care.

Or "how you'd love
A child of mine" (?),
Only to find
Contraception pills
Inside Aspirin box.
Enough fooling around,
Go on pill taking
See if I care.

Money you spend
Not earned.
Stoned and raving
Beauty but skin deep
Chimney black tarred inside

Now go on false Princess
Spend what is left of your own.
Without me, without me!
Just in case you do not get it:

<table>
<tr><td>Ohne mich</td><td>Lebe wohl</td></tr>
<tr><td>Senza me</td><td>Asta la vista</td></tr>
<tr><td>Bez mene</td><td>Do svidanja</td></tr>
<tr><td>Au revoar</td><td>and farewell!</td></tr>
</table>

THE UNIVERSE

Whatever you see
Is there no longer
Moved elsewhere.
In constant motion
Nothing can stand
But spins, how it is
Hard to understand.

(2)Stars light years
From the Earth,
We watch in awe
Likely extinguished
White dwarfs by now
Nothing is as it seems
Galaxies by the zillion.

By Entropy law
Ever more disorder
Is Nature's way.
What laws then
Govern the path
Of single living cell
To a modern Man?

(4) Big Bang Theory
Postulates boldly
Expanding Universe
From a single dot
Into empty space
Slowing down.
No more no less.

Instead, we find
It expands forever
Faster and faster.
Left without answer.
We model Dark Matter,
Whatever that is it
Ought to explain
Paradox therein,
If little better than
Black Magic of old.

Sad fact is we are
Novices, Ignoramus.
If Science has not
The clues get into
Religion perhaps.
Mind you observer!

Hundreds of creeds
   Cannot all be right.
   Much more likely
They are all wrong.

   Thermodynamics
   Laws One Two Three
   They work on Earth
   In confined space
   Time on our scale
   What is outside of us
   Dimensions more
   Or worlds far beyond
   Only the Maker knows

THE BLACK DOG

How did I ever get here! Silence shrieks,
Darkness blinds. Colours merging
Melting away. Hair stands up andg
None can hear calls for help.
Welded fast to the ground
Bathing in sweat, arms of lead,
Now look!! There is the back dog
Menacing, snarling, fangs flashing,
Me, just meat in his way.
No way left out, but bite the bullet
And enter Darkness, stony silence at last

MEGA-POLIS

Re-bar bones
Concrete muscle
Sinew of glass
Heartless beast
Throws Maker
Sand in the eye
Gravity defiant
Colors all grey

The hungry beast
Clamors for height
Doped on clouds
And higher still
It gobbles down
Everything in sight
Grows like cancer
And sucks river dry

By three phase AC
Modern mega-polis
Spews out garbage
Belching air foul
All over for thanks
Bitumen for skin
Hemoglobin money
Red rim ball of fire

In the East
Already
Headless ants
On wheels
Frantically mill

In fruitless search
Of their long
Missing queen

SUBURBIA

You'd never guess how I love my 'burb
Given first chance I cannot wait to get away,
Hit the road and look for green pastures.
Give me cattle, sheep, blue sea, anything but
Brick veneer or sight of traffic lights.
Come weekend oh, what a blessing,
Get away early to avoid traffic jam.

And breathing exhausts that says 'cough!'
Having turned off home aircon buzzing
On expensive power, include the bonus:
Pure blessing to be away from the hoon
Teen's next door performing wheelies,
Or lawnmowers two stroke and four
Staccato horrible noise and blue smoke.

No sooner on the road, why does everybody else
Have the same stupid idea, bumper to bumper
Tempers build higher, 'move on you moron',
Shouts the driver behind frothing at the mouth.
Try dialing radio waves, talk back or Triple J,
Anything to beat the boredom, alas,
I cannot stand disc jockey, dare not say moo.

Oh, how we love our 'burb.
Against the odds after some distance put behind
Kids fighting still bored stiff on the back seat.
What should take minutes takes hours, more red lights
And another traffic snarl, we have not moved
Since the last traffic jam. The scene repeats itself
Over and over stop go, more stop than go in fact.

Hours later we arrive at last, half spent and exhausted
Limbs stiff needing urgently some blood circulation
Physical jerks or some suchlike pill for rejuvenation.
Then at last what we came for; the blue sea pops up in sight
Wow! Relief sighs all around alas, shock horror there is
Nowhere to park the crate. For that is all it is. Cost it may
An arm and a leg to run, petrol, insurance and fees.

Fees, deep down a box on four wheels
Glorified no end is what a motorcar is.
And then, just try living without one.
Hamstrung is the man from the 'burb.
Skillfully we manage to triple park
Legal it is nope, despite everyone doing it,
From a bush lawyer innocent by association.

Few hours baked in the sun,
Brine just as salty as last
Potato chips even greasier.
Before you can tell
Blinded by booby flesh,
On swaying hips, it is time
To head for beloved 'burb.

Fraying tempers ready to greet you.
Road rage and mid-finger up sign.
Bad mannered drivers young and old
Passing one on the inside.
Language coarse, foul and loud
All par for the course on the
Congested not so open road.

Modern cars can do double ton
Stuck for long stretches on idle
Denied in bottom gear crawling,

Radiators some unable to cope
With a hot day and air-con on,
Drive temp' dial beyond high H,
Performing like a steaming iron. - - -

Dark, street lights on
Back at home at last
After a hard day's yakka
Safe back in beloved suburbia,
All in one piece starving,
First stop fridge after
An eventful day it has been.

THE OAK TREE

Sweetest of words you whispered way back
How only can your laughter still resound?
Light that shone so brightly on your hair
Shoulder long; curled back in time space,
Can this be but a preservative canned dream?

Asked oak tree partner in crime for an answer:
Perched on the hill you'd have seen it old timer
Overlooking the bay, how many Oceans' waves
Had rolled in since smashed to smithereens,
Your roots can tell, can it be she is back?'

The answer arrives soon thereafter
Airborne on a puff of gentle wind
Rustling the leaves to a man in shadow
Of an oak tree crown patiently attuned
Struggling to hear heavenly messenger:

"Oh, your fickle creatures on the ground,
Discontented, busy always asking for that
You have cannot an' threatening me here
with chainsaw, blight, drought and tempest,
Just look at me content to stay where I stand."

 As if invited violent gust of wind
Out of nowhere pipes in the branches:
"Foolish man, don't ever let go of what
Has once been dear to your heart, now
Lonely pilgrim, and dare ask for it back."

Wind died as sun rose higher.
In tune with the oak tree with

Waves thundering on basalt ramparts
Serving time keeper of a different kind,
On the ground left, just me and the oak tree.

UNEMPLOYED

Black and white pictures dated 1929
Stare in your face again; just as then
Men regulation dressed clean shaved
Snake like wind all around CBD blocks

Centuplicate job applications mailed
In all directions, with stamps on all, but
Few if any replies in the mailbox
Just swallow hard there is no mail today

Subdued the queue inches forward some
Bodies wrapped in industrial deodorant
Anxious men for something to do shuffle
The feet play pocket billiard and chew gum.

Credit cards all screaming blood red
Savings history not so reprimands
Welfare knows them no longer and
Pockets empty not so the urge to spend.

Listening still? Shush off to planet X
Come back no more, just disappear
We do not want you on statistics here
Ditto do not ring up us we will ring you.

Years later nothing of substance changed
I fear to hold angry mob from barricades
before long there will not be jails enough
Nor hospitals to heal the gunned wounded.

DE-MO-CRA-CY (AUST.)

On summer vacations after many years
Back to the black stump cattle station
Where it had not rained a drop for donks
Young Bill is exchanging pleasantries
Seated at the brekky table
With his Pa busy fighting off
Drought flies and the Banks.
>   What tidings do yu bring?
>   From the big smoke, and
>   What fer heaven's sake these days
>   Did they drum into yu me young son?
>   It is costing pretty penny
>   While I can still afford it, I says
>   It had better be damned good?
De-mo-cra-cy you call it kiddo!
Ha, it sounds a good name for a Sheila, why
Those foreign woggy words here out of place!
Oh, Father protests young Bill, did you know
Aristotle, Homer, Pythagoras were,
Wogs as was Plato and Alexander the Great.
>   Did they breed Angus or Merino?
>   Fat lot of good
>   Objects Bill Sen. just
>   Ignorant peasants riding donkeys
>   And that settles it. Now eat your porridge and
>   No leftovers for De-mo-cra-cy to clean up, ha.
And the other purphy, animal rights you calls it.
Come with me back to the pigsty to show yu
Where the beacon you just ate came from. Remember Mitch
That porker you rode when here last?
That bacon and egg young Bill ate made him throw up and
Turned him thereafter into a vegan for life.

NOSTALGIA

Years later uninvited, back
to the scene of younger days,
alone, nostalgia driven I gaze
at shunned by Helios
monocolor grey autumn sky
of Northern Germany.

I gaze at the naked birch tree above,
branches stripped of leaves.
Disorderly like
a defeated army
weapons abandoned,
finished with History.

Silent traveler without a shadow cast,
I watch drab sparrows,
the only birds left here-about
pre-occupied with survival now and to-day:
subdued in no mood to chirp.

People on wheels rush about madly.
They remind one of disturbed ants
searching for the missing queen.
Uninspired just like the sparrows
few men find time for a note to chirp.
Citizen of sunny Australia, - - -

nostalgia driven,
nostalgia's dead,
what am I doing here?

A MONOLOGUE

Fritted away one day, pass an account
Of what is lost never to return!
Aye, painful enough that it is,
How much harder a task must be
To account for one's turbulent life.

Candle burning out on both ends.
And why is it when we do embark
Reminiscing on voyage through the past
Selected ports of call spring to the mind?

Cause not helped at all pleading
With Father Time to let one
Finish the work and the poem when
Short of empathy he scornfully rages:

> ***You have had a lend of me***
> ***Bone lazy pilgrim!'***

As if he cared what it takes
.To put bread on the table.
Roof over one's head, or
To spoil the one, he loves.

Spare a dollar for a rainy day,
No better, it consumes Time
Like starved elephants
Consume a fruit orchid.

This said one can delve
on brighter moments
When heart smiling
Wings were gained.

When one felt weightless
Lifted by clarity of purpose.
Thus, do not expect this to be
Chronological order CV, but

QUESTIONS APLENTY

ANSWERS BUT A FEW.

Becalmed running on engine
Dar es Salaam port left astern
Single-handed idle for once observing
Equatorial shadow around my feet.

On a high in search for something novel
I stepped out of the shadow guided by
Rainbow colors of strong khat weed
Watching scenes returning from my past.

Numbed by endless African misery
Traveling back in time, frame after frame
What did I see?
Fleeting images, snap shots, an' more:

    Of sculptor's hands collecting post WW2
    Wiped out family's broken shards?-
A naïve idealist standing up to Communist dogma and rule?-
A young man down-under starting from down-under
indeed.–

    Or perhaps productive years in Africa
    Broken by more African wars of cca 1973?-
Image followed of a by-stander in 1992 Bosnian war
Rescued when out of ammunition trapped in deep snow?

    A white coat scientist
    busy with isotope distribution
    Pursuing research on
    Metabolism of Dope in Sport,

Back to boring suburban
drudgery of nine to five?-
Or writer of
Un-predictable moods

Who lost two octaves,
after vocal tumor.
This or the other,
I would be the last to know.

What I do know, having doubts
Is worms eating your insides.
Self-doubts born of attrition
And ocean of indifference.

Once more self-reflections returned of
A pilgrim at constant war within himself.
And wars without; burdened by restless mind
Stuck on the frontier searching.

For why and why and why my Lord
The Beast cannot live
And let live in peace?-
With more pain to follow:

Was he a foolish man
Willing to share his last?
Or poor imitations of Sinbad.
Who will be the judge?

Of so many promising starts
And indifferent endings asking:
'Should I have tried a lot harder?'
Faithful to a noble cause to the bitter end,.

Or just another
every-day scout
After gratification
and easiest way out?

A scientist, a sculptor,
A pilgrim, a writer, a sailor,
One and all or a comprehensive failure
And none of those.

And do personal accounts
Matter at all my Lord
In great scheme of things.
One or none who cares.

Is it at just navel gazing luxury
Because watching me depart
Bulging eyes focused on me
I remember was a black child.

Sucking on his thumb
For a taste of food.
Which star in Heaven only guides him?
In fable of level playing fields

Where the same slimy grease
Of the broth swims to the top
Immaterial by what
 -ISM suffix prefixed.

Daydreaming more
I ran into a tropical low
Stormy seas headwind calling for.
Storm jib hoist and changing tack, before,

Father Time standing in for Grand Inquisitor
Had me back on the wheel for more torment.
**"Confess, or more pain, confess, confess you must!
You should have accomplished much more, confess!"**

"Who knows Master of all Life and all Things?
You see Latin and Ancient Greek
Are not amongst crude languages I do command.
My past participle can appear in the wrong place.

Many of my adjectives may offend
Even unintended, with a hard edge.
Discriminating critics knives out
Hold all this an' more against me."

What they should not
Hold against me though' is
Colors nailed to the mast.
For I am a lone mariner.

In the wrong time zone naked,
Stripped of fancy clothes
Without a mask and pretense.
Common man's poet.

Of whites and blacks
A troubadour whose
Lute fallen silent since
Can no longer be heard.

Neither polish nor money
Ready to deceive

Can change the course.
Single-handed none on watch.

**Destined to end up
On a rocky shore.**

ANNO DOMINI MMXXI

All fame mimique; All riches alchimi/
The Sunne Rising by John Donne

Two Millennia it has been and more
And still, we wait.
For Your second coming we wait.
Pill intakes on the rise
Bones go brittle
Strides shorten
Eyesight weakens
And still, we wait
From cradle to grave.
Historians scribe in the interim
Without Legions at Your side
They fore-see with dread
Betrayal and crucifixion again.

Busy elsewhere, lo, who is muscling in!
Read the portal inscription in the temple
Patronage of the Golden Calf Monetarism is back again:
" There ain't such thing as dirty money.
You are worth bab' what money you've got
Not a cent more and everyone has a price."
Folks in debt that is all but the 1%
According to this worthless at best.
For this to be explain how come
We buried our brightest in the past
Over Centuries declared paupers?
Not one or two but most, end of story!

And if the workers' color blue and white were
Just another commodity to be scooped

By Banks too big to fail.
Like iron ore and wheat.
If the Oceans fished out were
Just another garbage dump with falling pH.

If value there was none in pristine clean river, or
Air free of Hydrogen Sulfide and smog
Fit to breathe, you lot can stick your credo
Where it belongs and eat your ill begotten money!

And then as if they knew not
We resent mocking humbug.
Ach, "Land mine merchants be ashamed!"
Ach, "Amputees to fly first!" I return serve.
Or the pious chants from the war mongers
In the front pew we are captive audience to:
Ach, "Forgive us the Merciful Lord (!),
We knew not they had no WMD."
I hope He runs out of Mercy! Amen."

Computer chips guide us, not Memories.
In marshy sand footings feel insecure.
Forced to search for footsteps You left,
All in vain we cannot find them
Obliterated by Saharan wind Simoun.
Commandments You gave Moses
Fading out too, growing fainter and fainter.
For ears plugged up with industrial noise.
What is left nowadays to guide the masses?

Of Eden between Euphrates and Tigress
True to Homo sapiens form Hell remains
And tumbling church spires.
Much of what we touch we debauch
Used and abused into Bank accounts.

Garbage dumps the destination. - - -

For how much one man can take free
At the cost of many stranded mouths open?
How much closer my Lord
Must be the Judgment Year?
Just do not leave it for another MMXXI,
Or there may be but a few judged fit
To meet St. Peter at the Pearly Gates.

COLLAR WHITE

Lex uno ore omnes alloquitur

Australia, land of big droughts, and floods
Whose billionaires' tax exempt sleep easy
And only PAYE lambs pay Income tax.
Where Taxation avoidance a' la USA,
Flourishes like Lucerne after rain and
Remains the main industry left in town.
Where a bank robbery means a different thing
And badge of honor is white collar crime.

It was said: "Some people rob you with a six gun
Others with a fountain pen."
Oh, it has never been good,
Now worse it has ever been
Since the days of Al Capone.
Myriads of acronyms starting with ASIC
Do not mean a thing and ASIC (sick) all right
Is just sand in the eye, as in Courts of Law:

"Face up to your crime!"
His Worship sternly demands.
Avarice your second name,
Sentences to come on your head.
Millions you defrauded from poor folks
 Unambiguously clear the evidence, -
And then, inn't a cryin' shame,
Such a resourceful clever chap.'

'Your Warship, the offence can be excused,'
Defense QC pleads with poise self-assured,

'My client he wears collar white,
Victim of mitigating circumstance.

A piddling street mugger, a pocket picker? Oh no,
No, Your Worship, but a man of substance is my client,
Whose profligate de-facto shot through. As aforesaid, the class,
the color he wears whiter than white.'

.......Court adjourned for two months....

HOW TO MEASURE THE PAIN?

When lightning strikes
tinder dry bush
Fire breaks out
to consume
Life in its path.
Days later nothing but
charred remains, yet
months later Life returns
in green shoots.

Nature orders
a beginning and
an end to everything.
Except to depravity and
endless human misery;-
And then, just how
to measure the pain.

Decibels to quantify the noise.
Kilograms the mass.
Meters for linear distance,
but pain?
What unit to quantify the pain.

Maybe a JOLT would do. If so
how many jolts does it take
to send one around the bend,
and how many more
to break one's heart.
And why a handful of Banksters
own just about everything?

RAGA OF SEVEN VIRGINS

Bunker oil boilers feed non-stop
ship's propeller shaft turbine and hot it is
even in icy Polar seas, greasy and smelly.
Hotter on just an average day and
hot as Hell in Tropics
where seamen inside
roast oven called engine room
service the hungry beast's bowels.

> Torn away from banks of Brahmaputra
> never once to Monrovia home port
> tramp ship a home it cannot be
> albeit it is all these men have got.
> Homesick to Hindu bone marrow
> crews chew on rotu, while their Muslim
> vegan soul
> settles for a plate of fried noodles
> Watching Dakar or Chittagong news.

Tramp steamers
disgorge loads of
whatever to wherever whenever
a contract bid trumps.
Crew rewards slim indeed
forced to skimp a meal
in order to compete, and
Bangla Dashi only need apply.

> Auto pilot set on rhumb line
> tramp ships navigate through
> teeth of hurricane; enough churn to turn
> your insides out, or worse, made to punch
> rolling like a stuck pig into savage Force 12
> at ¾ speed battling to deliver cargo on time.

And then, on days when Sun smiles for forgiveness.
When more plastic garbage is tossed astern overboard, you will find
crews still in their pajamas on their backsides in rhythmic unison
merrily chipping away
rust on vacant top deck.
Chanting over and over and over again
the raga of Seven Virgins
as the legends of old promise silk veiled prostrate
willing and able in seaman's paradise.

                    Bearings worn out,
                    rust having eaten of hull its fill,
                    rudder pintles clapped out,
                    like a sex worker after lipstick
                    no longer sticks,
                    after war paint peels off,
                    after having served its purpose
                    retirement day certain, your home come
                    steamer is off to wrecking grave yard.

More Bangla Dashi moustache
swarm over dismembered hulk
oxy torch and ball chain at work.
Brutal end of a line, a demise
on sticky shores of Bay of Bengal under
110 Fahrenheit in the shade
humidity at dew point
never you mind
and no safety talk.
Just in case you should ask:
Aye Capt'n, what about them crew?
                    "Sent off in this fable of marvelous economy,
                    (you do not say!), to compete
                    on level playing fields with next batch
                    of desperadoes willing to sign for less.
                    Pittance for severance pay

no pension, no bonus,
just take your triptique
then tip toe quietly into the dark night."

And to think
merchant seaman
like many others
used to be
a well-paid job
one you could
bank and build
a future upon.

QUACKS VS. BITERS

Attired in plumes and feathers white
Grounded they ungainly
Stagger and swagger about
On three pronged two red feet.

To carnivores all one and the same
Best roasted
On charcoal grill,
But wait there a millisecond!

Ducks quack,
Ducks fly low,
Ducks get shot,
For trophy or the pot.

Geese fly high
In bomber squadron formation.
Geese when under attack
Bite and fight back

Advocate of all Life
Feathered finned
Or otherwise
I score geese well ahead.

SHE IS A HE IN ACTS THREE

Act1.
Wine waiter Miguel practicing broken French
pirouettes around mahogany table for two
decked with porcelain and silver cutlery.
> Under Hilton chandeliers beaming
> bundled light photons to four corners
> all novelty splendors to seated Markus
> Country six foot five Footy forward star.

Crimean caviar, Meum champers on ice and a five course
gargantuan meal on offer when one course would do.
Pleasantries, more on the way to freshman Mark as
she whispers sweet words of unbridled passion
Punctuated with: "give your wallet a rest Darl'."

Act2.
Inside the apartment she dims the light
and she dims it some more
Mark on his back there wandering why
It takes so long to peel off clothes.
> Then the wig falls off, she turns into him;
> long eye lashes, manicured toe nails
> Dior perfume and ounces of Aurum
> sporting a black eye all for dross.

Horny to placid in a millisecond
Mark panic stricken jumps out of bed
clothes collected running for the fire escape.

Act3.
At nightshift portiere desk
scene unfolds: Mandy is Andy.
"Yes Maam, oops, Yes Sir,
let me fetch the Rolls,
valet will be here in a tick."

She, oops, he returns in tears:
"I hired the Rolls what a fool, then picked
Footy forward straight as a ruler; get me a cab
for a single day, enough damage has been done"

THE WAR

Nietzsche: Wish to Power
You have made your way from a worm to a man
And much of you is still a worm.

War is not turned on and off by a toggle switch
War is deliberate act of a power hungry deviate.

War winners are few with spoils
And losers many like modern Economy.

It does not stop with peace treaty signed
War goes on forever for those who lost.

It is still on when a widow reads worn out yellow pages
Sent from the front by the one who never came back

War is on when orphan eyes focused on a wall photograph
Wants to say -look here father, I am your son.

War is still on when those fortunate to return
Talk softly in a different mono-syllable tongue.

And war is still on when those tilling land
Trigger off a land mine limb blown off.

AGNES DEI #2

(..and blessed shall be the meek...
...and the weak shall inherit the Earth...)??

'Wake up you dormant spirits' Heavens called
Let us hear the trumpets sound and the horn
Heralding the new born!

A child born in manger
To change the World
For now, and forever.

His birth marks the Time
Into Millennia
For now, and forever, amen.

Sadly, oh Lord before next amen
It must be said Thy teachings
Do not seem to work on planet Earth.

Forgiven time and again Barbarian
Enemies hold us for fools and
We have no more cheeks to turn.

WORN OUT MIRRORS

Timid hearts struggle to coin true words,
Never to leave our lips drowned in Decibels of
Perfumed sales pitch and traffic noise.-
Other words are spoken in bad faith,
When done to us we call it lies! Let me ask:
"Does it all matter; after all, you are who you are?"
        White woman for hours captive
        At beautician's parlor day-dreams
        Of short hair curly black and fuzzy, while
        Black girls in the slums spend
        The rent money so they can boast
        Hair shoulder long like a Whitey.
           You are who you are, where is the point
           All that lacquer, mirrors and war paint?
Face lift, Botox; a fifty year old flattered
She looks 25. Hmm? Sales talk surely.
Same frail body, still old tired eyes and
Brittle old brittle bones. *Why do we pretend to be*
Who we are not, and want to acquire such as
We have cannot.And does it matter?
        It is all for dross, you are who you are
        Beauty but skin deep flattered by worn-out mirrors.
        And while grinding world beckons myopic Dons
        Sweet music is traded in for deafening noise.-
        From ashes to ashes, expiring license to mess about.
        From a drop of rain to a brook, rivers to oceans beyond.
        From stellar carbon chain you and me, round and round
        Waste there is none except greed vanity and wars.
Around the corner dark retribution lurks,
Smoldering farms and burning homes.
Open mouths crowding slums and thirsty throats.
Tell young ones to be afraid, good Hope is forlorn,

Capable of a change for the better we seem not,
We try to make amend, alas, at the wrong end.
After all we are only and can ever be
Who we are and what a tragedy that is!

FANTASIA

Alone I sit by the shore tuned in to
Asthmatic bored the Pacific Ocean.
Rolling back the years until
Reaching a black cavern wall.

Carried yon the blue horizon I begin to wonder
About intractable complexities of Life
And who and why would not want to figure out
What washes up with the next high tide?

For one, names we have for things one can
Smell touch and taste, and things abstract
Fantasia in one's head; peace of mind
No money can buy; what little joy there is left tax free.

JSB's Mass in C I hear with no-one nearby.
Sound none except the organ chords exploding in my mind,
Consumed in greedy state of bliss I decide to
Keep state of Nirvana all to myself.

SHEPHERD SOLDIER TIM

(I)   When the bugle called the retreat, it found
Soldier boy Tim the last one who stood for his platoon.
Others in agony left behind stranded inside barbed wire
Pumped full of German lead. A senseless order it was to attack
For no good purpose, and worse, Tim's Lady Luck deserted
Put to task to explain how so the only survivor.

(II)   Boy of sixteen drafted to make up diminishing numbers
Once shepherd, Tim from the High Country
Stands attention in blinding rain for hours on end
Body cold and wet to the bone wearing
Heavy steel helmet that got more killed than ever saved.
Shrunk wet leather straps biting into skin, yet
The only thing to keep the eyes dry.

(III)   "Two steps forward!" The order comes defiantly ignored.
Private Tim frozen in time listening instead to his heartbeat.
Enraged MP Sarge growls at the point of a loaded gun:
"You ignorant peasant cowardly scoundrel,
Methinks we will have to teach you a lesson,
Now back to solitary confinement on the double!"

(IV)   A week later back in the Military Prison courtyard
Hot sun shone at Private Tim a shepherd once upon a time with
Parched thirsty throat about to fall off his feet.
"Two steps forward!" A familiar order came and ignored.
Once again, boy soldier Tim just stood there frozen in time.
"Back to the solitary! The MP Files raged out of control.

(V)   No more to be gained by punishment alone
Private Tim is sent to re-join the raging battle on the front line.

Upon inspection found not to have fired a single bullet.
"" When is all this industrial killing going to stop!"He dares ask.
Top Brass got to hear, just imagine if more acted like this!
Court-marshal passed the sentence: Deserter to be shot at
first daylight.

(VI)   Times change, not at all proud of killing their own
The Army steadfastly maintains deserters were weeded out.
He might have been only sixteen when drafted

FROM KISSES TO SHRAPNEL

Smoldering ruins overhead
Platoon's last man fit to fight on
Re-counts kisses mailed from home telling him
Somewhere yond people still sleep well and sleep in bed.
Until artillery barrage turns night into day again
And Love she sent sealed with tears remains
The last pillar of hope within man-made inferno of
Blood, shrapnel and bricks falling all around.

Those bricks upon a brick once
A home would have been and
Soldier next to another soldier in step
Army on the march; down the lane into
Army's cemetery and cancelled dog tags
For Many who once proudly marched.-
No more than a hint of mere folly remains
Exposing the Few in the HQ
Who sacrificed the Many.

Snowflakes sprinkled in the hair and
Mountain dew misting in the eyes.
Burdened down by heavy war trauma
weighing over her slender shoulders
a war widow watches a mute boy returned soldier
Uncertain if brick upon a brick is still a home
And if that bird song could be for real but
For that twinkle in Mum's eyes.

THE OLD WITCH

Once upon a time children, a dreadful noise I heard
Under full Moon-lit night sky manned by a witch of old.
A ramjet powered broom stick she rode for a steed,
Piloting in acrobatics the night skies uncontested.
       Clear as bell for an instant I saw overhead
       Under witches' hat in charcoal black face
       Menacing King Cobra's hood and eyes
       Glow of emerald green. More to her face still
       Front teeth choppers of a harmless rabbit.
       Before I froze in fear, trust me, I heard
       A shrill voice pierced the night; easy to tell
       Fury imported right from the gates of Hell.
A comprehensive ball of terror
To anyone in breach of WTO rules
She would slam any brazen offender
No hesitation here or mercy on offer
Into the baking oven for roast dinner.
       And yes, little children,
       CEOs in them days
       Behaved in exemplary fashion
       Like good children would, for most part anyway.
       Alas, my readers would have under: "what next?"
       Already have guessed unraveling a twisted plot
       And one wholly unexpected.
Out of fodder the old witch shriveled
With time starved
Then in bed she died.
None is there to patrol the scene any more overhead
On large scale goods are dumped and taxes avoided.
Pollies wink, they shake hands with all and sundry
       Smug smiles from ear to ear; bedrock of bastardry.

Enough hot wind here to make the icebergs
thaw,
Stock market calls encores to a jolly good show.
Shame about the unemployed basking in
memories
Of the old WTO witch and their forever lost jobs!

DIMMING SUN

"Hi", passed his lips,
"Hello", came back,
"Long time no see",
Lovers once
Sparring tit for tat

Planets, they orbit since
Diverge around
A dimming sun
Hungry for warmth
That never comes.

Starved for attention
Cat and a dog they search
For company ersatz
Safety first
The worry is

Dimming sun may somehow
Cause sunburn.

FORD PREFECT 1952

Ol' granny at 95 can drive new auto Mercedes Benz.
    just for fun try driving my old crate,
  jumping out of second and no hand brake.
  I manage her all right; see how far you get.

On the flat she chugalugs along all right, simply fine,
  come a hill side climb a different story.
  Double clutch all the way down to first
    rev her up till tacho shifts off scale.

  She grew on me, like one of the family,
  the old girl sticks out in a crowd somewhat
of distinct character. Spares mighty hard to find
forced to improvise. Holden clutch and Jap 'electrics
well done none can tell, stuff all the difference.

  Pride of the place, hard to part with
  grown onto you just like one of the family,
some question why care and money more be spent
  on her not without vices. She likes to run hot,
    capricious at other times, smokes a fair bit
and is hard to start, not to mention awful fuel economy,
  so what, the veteran old beauty Ford Prefect 1952.

CITY THAT NEVER SLEEPS

Expelled from Eden, torched in Sodom
tossed into caldron to stem molten iron.
Wars ad infinitum and back damaged goods,
uprooted from Carthage and Troy
bruised Adam builds a den of sin,
a city that never sleeps where anything goes.

With craving of a drug addict a beast is born.
Morals of a hyena looks and polish to deceive.
Love for no other than easy money.
Visitors call in from far and wide.
Curious by-standers for most part
walk the streets paved with fools' gold
in a city that never sleeps and anything goes.

Waiters, cabbies' good workers all
mill around the table for crumbs that fall.
A market place has flesh for sale
perfumed in industrial deodorant.
Drunks and junkies staggering about.
Arm of the Law on remote control out of sight.
Commerce rules here, pimps and whores
in place just like your grocery stalls,
in a city that never sleeps and anything goes.

Bright neon lights flash on and off,
giant magnets drawing men like moths
with equal outcomes. Suddenly the master switch
trips off on transformer failure unexpected.
Power to drive the beast no longer on tap,
magic of city that never sleeps but a delusion.
Glow in dark night at 2 AM down to

that of the whites in scared men's eyes,
jumping cue calling taxi, taxi (!),
in a city that never sleeps and anything goes.

ATHEIST

By mere chance we are here
is that what you like to believe.
That what you see just so happens:
the world spinning like a roulette.
Win some lose some,
and who cares.

Billions of living cells
functioning in perfect unison
so horribly complex
it can never be half understood,
much less duplicated.
All by mere chance.

Then what glue holds
the fabric together.
If it is as you proclaim,
how can one cell having gone bad
see you in palliative care
defeating a billion good ones?

Which statistics my numbers man
you care to name explains that?
When ignorance
and arrogance
walk hand in hand,
give yourself a re-think.

Without a Master and ways
we may never get to know,
how can this world
function at all.

Or is that like the rest
of your credo.

Nothing out of nothing,
for nothing
worth nothing
into nothing,
all in vacuum
and who cares?

WHEN WILL I SEE YOU AGAIN

Airbus 320 gains altitude
doing simply fine
it is me out of control
heart left behind
on the ground
of my old homeland

Mljet island pearl
in the Adriatic
loves of innocent youth
those who shared
my smile and bread

when will I see you again

YOURS TRULY

From Mark to Jennifer
Jennifer to Henry
Henry to Carmen
Carmen to Josh
Josh to Martha
Adam to Steve
round and round
some names are
clearly left out
it is for update 1.2
thanks, a heap for
warm hospitality
it has been good
to know you and
see you around

Yours truly,
Bacillus Gonorrhea.

LOTUS EATERS 2020

It occurred to me to test my friends
play God for a day and what would your decrees be
 Abolish poverty
 cure every disease
 find parents for the orphaned
 make young ones obey
 arts and poetry bloom
 shame the rich into sharing
 or let it just be and leave it
 to HM King to ponder

All eyes on me ha ha
what magic would I conceive
 make water run uphill
 old men grow horny again
 bed rodent and feline together
 abolish small talk and gossip
 or hardest task of all
 make sweet love
 last forever

Pull my leg comedians all you like
on day one I would
 have molten tanks and canons
 cast into plough shears and spades
 submarines and warships scuttled
 make reefs for fish to breed
 drive some sense into folks
 to stop breeding like rodents
 macho men still keen to wage war
 have dispatched to the front line
 face the ugly enemy eye to eye

This I would try do not tell me you critics
it is all hog wash, or that strange voice
        I heard again whisper in a dream
        unravel fading out of tune
        'More stars than grains of sands
        why lotus eaters still convinced
        you are the flavor of the Universe—
        A sugar ant hero to his nest
        climbed all the way to the top of a grass blade
        studiously scanned the horizon
        saw no other kind around, then proclaimed
        we must be the Master of the Universe

How old would one be never to age
if reborn with new eyes every day
How fast could one run if never feet had
to touch solid ground
How rich would one be if for every cent spent
two fell from heavens - imagine
what would you tell the greedy banks
How if when and then just fill in the gaps my man

        If mindless destruction you can watch
        chew gum and not be incensed
        if you can walk past a hungry child
        salivate while munching on your cake
        if observe crushing poverty you can
        sing a song and pretend it is a mirage
        your heart has a dollar sign in front
        If and when how and then just fill in the gaps.

Why me or why worry about world sick
in palliative ward care on morphine
gone off the rail how can little me make a difference

why Heavens above do not come down on henchmen
who am I to judge 'sweet nothing to do with me'
says who 'just walk on steady look the other way'
Why and if and when and then just fill in the gaps

       Step forward two steps backwards
       males once men stare idly into nothingness
       observe robots and coolies take over while
       smarty-pants economists call it progress -
       how come we are stuck in the same place
       One day at a time spent before you know
       the sun rises where it did twelve months ago

The same sun, place the same time and rut
except it is on who can dish out more smut
ra-ra and gaga twins rule the airways
it is just as warm and a year's gone
One on one is one by one over one into one
if still one when and then just fill in the gaps

WHEN THERE ARE TWO INSIDE OF ONE

When bayonet up
the Hard one hollers:
'*Chaaargeee* in! kill the Hun,'
while the Softy petrified
inside browned uniform
declares it is bedlam.

When the Hard one demands:
'Strangle the cheating bitch,
an eye for an eye, and
a tooth for a bloody tooth,'
but Softy refuses,' Love is blind,
turn the other cheek'.

When the soft one overcome
with full *tummy* guilt remorse
donates to walking starved African
while the hardnosed one claims:
'It's too late can't you see St Joe Blow,
for them, all hope is lost'.

Dichotomy, split personality,
psychoanalysis (?), no, no and no,
does it not prove though
even the Almighty Father
in the Heavens above
can botch up a design job?

WHY MY LORD

Not blue as Strauss' waltz would have it,
brown artery detritus laden river Danube
drains Panonian plains to the Black Sea
under autumn sky of lead and sorrow.
Emissaries of death flock of hungry ravens
stalk on the ground; North wind pipes acrid
gun powder smoke along the upturned ground,
wailing tune in time to cannon fire
prelude to winter snow bitter cold.

Wars come and go, exhaustion of combatants
peace but an interim; it is October 1991 AD
Romeo last man standing fearing capture
worse than death itself, no help in sight
resigned to fate he watches the timeless river,
eddies close to shore, fish jump and
smoldering ruins of Vukovar left behind.
Those images growing fainter and dimmer.
He knows he will never see Sun rise again.

In final act of defiance, having blasted
two Serbian M72 tanks to iron scrap
and more clanking in line behind,
the last bullet left for himself
he puts it to the Master in the sky,
***does true love forever I promised Julia
also, must die; what have I only done to You
to punish me thus, why or why, can this be
all you have in store for me after promise of liberty.***

Lord Ares on heavenly roster duty thunders:
'Your insolent fool for liberty barter blood

we must have war, do you not understand,
how else could one sell weapons.
Stop hungry mouths multiplying
like rabbits or lemmings,
keep factories busy, or acquire
someone else's oil water and land!'

DAY'LL COME AGAIN

Day will come again when pension funds are broke,
when none will toss out bread
'cause it's a day old a little hard to chew.
When to be just left in peace
to soak up sun will be all we dare ask.

Day will come again when facing violence of war
we will fondly remember memories of being bored.
When one who talks loudest
sells the biggest lie when it becomes official
there are too many of us and too old.

Day will come when the rich hide behind barbed wire,
guards with machine guns mounted on watch tower.
When shirtless masses once again
in pool of blood storm, the barricades.
This day I fear may be closer than many think.

WRIT BY WHOM?

Poems that stir the soul
make heart miss a beat
and one's eyes go dewy.
Writ by a committee or consensus?
Never so my brethren.

By a discussion of learned friends,
Politicians, businessmen or
merry party going hoi polloi?
By a joint team effort perhaps?
Never so my brethren.

Go and search though
amongst the underprivileged,
soldiers sick of killing, or loners
in solitude along seldom trodden paths.
There you may find your bard.

VULTURES OF THE APOCALYPSE

Gate crushing uninvited
mounted on metallic birds
vultures of the Apocalypse
descend from the sky.
A napalm whirlwind strikes.
Here they are one minute, gone,
disappeared the next, behind smoke,
dust and flames of smoldering huts.
Left for dead behind the curse
from heavens in tears,
are dying women, infants
and burned old men.

Builders, teachers, fishermen
farming folks,
builders and providers,
we need them all.
Could not do without them.
Not the savage brutes
though, whence only
do they come from?
Vultures of the Apocalypse
under which plume and banner
fly their metallic birds.
Who is their Lord Master?

Stars and stripes insignia
thirst for Kill Count dispatch
creation of Lucifer high on dope.
Where indeed is the home

of the vicious breed?
Hidden in the cumulus clouds,
fields of tall wheat perhaps,
the deep blue sea, in jungle forests,
in bowels of molten earth,
Lord's grand design of Hell on Earth,
Or Pentagon, Washington DC, USA?

LOVE #1

Like a motorcar
filled with petrol
how long you will drive
before the big E
calls flashing red
to some extent
depends largely
upon yourself.

Push your own ends,
aside everyone else's,
and you will find
petrol's gone
in next to no time.
'cause volatile
just like petrol
is so called love.

The all-consuming fire
of marriage day one
over the years burns out
to mere flicker pilot light,
later down the line beaten
into a submission as
any divorcee will
readily recognize.

A NEW BORN

Blessing to us in the West
is a new born child,
more a burden
to an African Mum
leading ten more
struggling behind
mouths choking
with Saharan sands
shoes fallen
to bits somewhere
along the never ending track.

A Lottery in Life
most will agree
one cannot choose
the parents
nor the country of birth.
List of all
what the future holds.
**Forget all politicians and
economists boldly project
if done with a straight face
and not in jest!**

FOOT STEPS LOST IN SAND

Footmarks You left in sand
at beginning of our time
we would gladly follow had not
Simoun the Saharan wind
hidden them from our eyes
and covered them forever.

The Commandments You decreed
echoing on the wings of Simoun
grow ever fainter, too faint now
for our feeble powers of hearing,
a handy excuse for transgressing.
Take Euphrates and Tigress paradise.

Inherited, now only a hell remains
and tumbling church spires.
Whatever we touch we debauch,
for how much one man can take,
all cost free ahead of many, and
how close must be the end my Lord.

NATURE'S CLOCK

Back to innocence of youth
in another time and place
of desires as they were
long since faded.
Faces, memories forgotten, so
why do we want to remember?
Roll on, roll in, smash to spray
call the next wave and the next.

Under a patch of blue sky
gulls claim their own,
tide rolls in as it has done
twice a day for eons.
It is more than trivia, back to
roll on, roll in, smash to spray
another wave and the next.

Never fail it is another wave
each one though slightly different
hard lands to spray; so passé
so many other pressing tasks to fill
should one have to mention this?
Roll in, roll on, smash to spray
one more wave and the next.

We toil and strain, day in day out
for all that, the gulls take no notice.
Unimportant is man in scheme of things.
The sea not man times the tides and
sunrise as it has for billions of years.
Roll in, roll on, smash to spray
the beautiful thing,

*the next and the next
and nothing a man can do
can change any of that.*

A TRAVELLER

Mountains lakes and seas
I have crossed.
Traveled millions of miles
over desert and snow fields,
yet after all those years
nowhere does my shadow remain.
Oh Lordy, was it just an
ego Odyssey all in vain?

Faces of people wearing smile
I can recall.
Hear voices of others
no longer around.
A long journey has it been
and ongoing, for one
born under a wandering star
final station next call remains.

Those who refused to share my bread,
'cause besides brown eyes,
my name read all wrong,
I do not remember them.
Having learned to soak up winter sun
and share in fun, perhaps
my meandering ways and travels,

it was not all in vain.

FILTHY LUCRE

'Arms merchants going hungry
and pigs will fly', you say.
Landmine merchants seated
in cathedral's front pew pray:
'Forgive us Almighty.',
'Pigs will fly before He does', I hope.

A word to those who proclaim:
'One's worth what money
you have got and not a cent more.
Greed is good, never is enough.
Broke you are worth a naught
including some rich gone broke.'

If greed is good how come
we are sunk in filthy debt,
all broke except the 1%.
Why are the land and seas
used as garbage dumps.
So, stick your ideology.

Right up your buns.
If all the world was obsessed
sick with money as you are,
it would stop dead in its tracks.
We buried our brightest
in the past paupers.

Not one or two
but most.

ATLANTIS

Earliest of free thinkers, first of
such denizens to walk this Earth.
Art teachers of Minoans and Thrace,
where you blue eyed, short or tall?
Fame that lives to this day
if only by word of mouth
what splendor and inspiration!

Was it you, or the Phoenicians
who created stunning Astarte,
the loveliest Goddess of Love?
She, who drove men crazy enough,
to jump ship, desert the ranks,
forsake wife, brood and home.
Where only upheavals of Earth buried you.

Or was it island sunk into abyss?
Given latitude and longitude alone,
we would dig up mountains
we would drain a sea to find
what remains of supreme
work of Arts and your marbles.
Oh, before I sign off.

What galleon ships did
Atlantis fleet command,
sails black or white, and why
only word of mouth remains.
Will we ever find out,
Unless it is but a myth
Something does not add up.

WHITE HERON

Snow white plumes grace divine
heron forages amongst garden worms.
Gone off sea food, sick or persecuted,
Or fish all up and gone
the most likely cause?

Descending on olive grove
flock of hungry gulls' squawk
picking off green fruit
unheard of in the past.
Bells, scarecrows and gardeners
up in arms defeated they give up.

While close inshore undersize fish
drowned in nets of death
kilometer long end dumped
overboard. Pox on the mankind!
Whatever we touch turns to garbage.

Free animals out there we
dare call wild had they ever trust in us
it has been betrayed untold times,
and abused, we the enemy
and do not they know it.

White heron focuses on me:
'Beware of smiling creature
tempting you with tit bits.'
A step closer it takes off
greeting me with distrust.

BEZERKISTAN BOSNIA

Travel Northern Bosnia roads
a generation after civil war
pass villages empty of people
charred remains of hospitals
weeds growing ten feet tall
in wheat fields of pre-war.

Of fools we will never be short
you hear the self-admission
again, and again, politicians
up front with no idea where to
turn next. UN, ECC et all,
been there, done that, it was
and remains Bezerkistan.

Symptoms of mental disease,
sadistic minds off Richter scale,
penchant for cushy living
at others toil and expense.
Grab what you neighbor
took a life time to build
you do not have to save.

Sell his daughter to a slave camp,
rape the wife at gun point
taking turns, make sure
he gets the message never to return.
Cushy living at others expense,
from a small time, piddle crook
to Serbian hero in Bezerkistan.

A RETIREE

How did I only
end up here
on puny income
and bored stiff
for something
worthwhile to do

Had I sailed
closer to the wind
in hay days of old
spoke less
and nodded more
used the System
as most do

Would I have ended
in the same place
struggling to make
ends meet
counting cents not dollars
is a question
that bugs
some retirees

ROMANCE I

How many years to eternity?
That is how long it seems
Since I last held you in my arms.
Free man once more, at the wharf
Waiting for the island ferry to dock.
Sun's well up throwing diamonds
In spades around the waterfront.
Aquarelle scenery fills the eyes.
Gulls, pigeons and hawkers
Mingle with sense of purpose
For something to snatch.

Amongst cars and more cars
Are passengers queued to embark.
Locals and tourists fused as one
In commercial hassle bustle
Of a ferry disgorging masses
Forward —reverse pandemonium.
Still, I cannot catch a glimpse of you.
It takes so long! Or am I wrong?
My head's spinning in confusion.
Is the date correct, was I hearing right?
Or did you have a late change of heart?

Dark doubts threaten to eat my insides.
Then at last that short cheerful step
That gave you away despite
Dark sunglasses and Panama hat.
I knew it had to be you. -
As I held you in my arms
Dark clouds disappeared
With inane ideologies out the door.

Was that your or my heart racing?
Or both beating in unison?
From the darkness return to the land of living.

THE BIRD

On the thermals the albatross glides.
Aye big bird, how high can you fly?
Me on the ground close to ant nest
Envious left alone and earth bound.

Aye big white bird, how high can you fly,
If you could read my thoughts, would you
Let me be your pal and let me be airborne
To fly with you if only so in my thoughts.

On your wings I should not be heavy.
We would be heading for the Sun higher
And higher like Ikarus son of Deadalus,
Circling higher and higher sky bound.

My feathery friend how high can you fly?
High enough to escape this cruel world
Or just to lose sight of it for a while? -
Oh, can you still see me on the ground?

FATHER TIME

Raging storm lashed the freezing night
    Lightning and thunder, oh what a might.
I sat at my dinner table sharing company
    With a glass of wine and idle melancholy.

        Lights went out, thereafter I cringed in fear,
            Rickety timber stairway groaning in strain,
        I heard sounds of steps approaching here,
            Heavy metallic steps clanking in refrain.

Who goes there'? I feebly called out,
    Friend or foe don't mess here about.
Wait and wait no answer came; when
    Knock, knock, knock on the door began.

        Try to get up I did without success
            As if glued to chair in distress. —
        Next, I watched him walk right in
            Door closed bolted shut all in vain.

Him shimmering alight on inner fire
    I found myself drained of earthly desire.
Who could it be? How would I know
    Our visitor barging in from world below.

        "Helios the Sun God sends me here",
            He thus spoke floating above ground.
        I looked up in awe, my Lord Miserere
            What caused Thee to roam around?
In pain I gathered courage some and
    Decided but foolishly to make a stand.

"Why Father Time, what did I do to earn
    Thy anger, displeasure—and disdain?"

        "Ask not what you did", said He, "but what
            In many years of long life, you did NOT."
        "Help me Father Time I begged once more
            To comprehend why more ire than before."

Said He: "Do not think of it dark and grim,
    Before I leave it will, all be clear my pilgrim.
Because wherever you see me well ahead,
    Fear not the Grim Reaper dares not tread."

THE VOICE

Your voice is there with me
It echoes from the cabin walls
It pleads with me surging with the
Gale and rides the wild ocean crests
Leading me The Monsoon Drifter
Only the good Lord knows where

The voice wakes me up at night
Telling me Your hand is still there
In mine in our web of emotions
That new no earthly boarders
When You was I and I was You
And neither knew what that meant

And though You are world away
Your voice remains my guiding
Light helping me find the way
In search of our lost youth
Through the labyrinth of Pain
In the darkest of dark nights

(18.04deg S, 90.23 deg E)

ANCHOR SONG PREAMBLE

(HOMAGE TO RUDYARD KIPLING)

Somewhere up in the sky is a bard musing with the Lord.
A tall man unbending, -true soldier, an' sailor, one and all.

A word or two for a landlubber city bound
Versed not in Navy speak of old sea hound:
    'Turn the groaning capstan round an' round again,
    Over to *starboard bowser,* pull in that anchor chain,
Ahoy, heave the *bowsprit a peak*; -turn and turn ye once more'.
I' takes muscles aplenty an' willing deck-hands crew beside
To free the anchor *flukes* out o' mud against the run-out tide.

Stuck fast i' mud, bodies straining' muscles taut an' aching'
'Winch   that   bloomin'   iron   a   *peak*',   calls   the
coxswain prodding'.
    Shoulder to shoulder next to other men, all on the ball,
    Hardest part behind, hear the sweet clanking of *the pawl,*
In place to stop the heavy anchor chain falling back
and all
Till *the anchor's butt* is in, stowed in the *starboard hawser,*
Washed an' free o' mud, the *cathead's* got no time to ponder.
Ahoy ye good men, let her fly, ahoy!

Free at last, the ship's got steerage none, toyed by wind an' tide
Ahoy, snatch the gasket, let the sail out fly, we are out for a ride.
    Cleat the *sheets fore and aft,* do not forget the *davit-guy!*
    Hit   the   open   sea,   get   her   under   way   an'   hoist   the
    bonnet laddie!
Mule sail to the Yank, 'xcept no mule ever rode this high u'
the mast,

Nor killed that many. 'Twixt I forget, set the course for *Mother Carey,*
Oh, ye on the *wheel,* she's with Poseidon an' Neptune goin' merry.

TIME

Money I am not, or else there would be no hungry poor.
    Bequeath me one cannot nor push me out the door.
You cannot fold nor bank me, ignore nor rush,
    It makes no difference the blue ocean or the bush.

    Owned by none, fourth dimension I am called.
        I wait for no man, flowing just like a stream, -
    Tomorrow today is yesterday's flicker of a dream,
        In the night sky ray of star dust shine and then:

For twenty long years of pain and glum,
    I could not as much as see my aging Mum.
Hammer and sickle had fallen over since.
    Fresh zephyr blew in for a while to rise
Fools we thought, hopes of freedom arrive.

    Alas, before the morning sun could lift the dew
        Jailers of old an' the masters *them's* on the rise again,
    Like Naples's Mafiosi of cathedral's shiny front pew.
        Back, revived, ready to pounce an' usurp the rein.

Mum she wrote last: 'Son, but for you overseas,
    I'd have starved, empty church but a hope forlorn,
Flicker of my candle light put out by the brutes,
    The old church sits them turncoats; all hope's gone,
An' widowed long I am, back to wearing black again.'

EPITAPH TO A BARD

Let me chat up one poet of the past,
Esq. Henry Lawson's spirit I would ask:
We will take you on a grand land tour,
be warned Henry before you demur,
what it used to be this land is not,
great brown land has changed a lot.

He latched on quick, nodded the head,
not a single word exchanged. It went on
from here on all day long. Henry and me
would silently pass thoughts, to and from.
It worked fine on the Bankstown line
about to board the same morn.

Where do we start, I needed to know,
"I'll leave that to you my Sydney pal,
it's your home, so you lead the show."
No arguments there, not many won
arguing with Henry at best of times
so, we boarded for Bankstown bound.

Suburban train left from Circular Quay
on the discovery tour of the metropolis,
where Henry knew every drinking hole
while writing for the Bulletin magazine.
Glued to the seat as our train took off
Passengers full and, southwest bound.

"I see the old coat hanger works fine".
"Yes, Henry a century longer it'll be

almost paid off". He looked around,
I watched him fondling the moustache.
"Oh, I get it, a blind Freddy can see
it's stuffed, the White Australia Policy."

"These days they come in all colors
yellow brown and brindle, some are
model citizens making a quid or two,
or Aussie dollars as it is called since.
Others, well the less said the better".
Henry: "You mean just like us mob."

> That is how he saw it fair and square
> never shy to speak out in the past,
> Henry of old, as quick as flash
> never to miss a trick, even in 2021
> riding the rattler in peak hour rush
> next to me on the Bankstown line.

> "Lingo of old Henry has changed
> as well, should anyone call you gay
> make double sure you understand.
> And when you hear: 'You guys'
> called out, it is Yankee importation
> for Jack and Jill plural, both in one."

I followed his eyes fixed on the
buxom woman standing in front,
arm up for a hold, the mini rock
revealing all. "I'll be blown mate,
if only I was not dead, I would jump out
of me skin." This passed Henry on.

> I looked up myself and red the tattoo.
> Struth, I kid you not in capital letters

Queen's English: PAY AS YOU ENTER,
fair dinkum, that is what it read; well,
so much empathy for the weaker sex.
"Apologies Henry I need to explain.

       You see we have the birth control pill,
       now they decide when a baby
       is to be born, or never to be born.
       By the way old sport, it is just the same
       up top, State Premiers mostly women now
       I am obliged to admit.

And if that's not enough Henry, why
we have Sheilas on the submarines."
"Stone the crows!" Henry protested.
"A bare bum and none does a mooo,
or a word to say, what is to become
of you? Where is the flamin'shame!?"

       "You might have been ladies' man,
       Henry, you ain't seen nothing yet.
       Do not go near a social club at night
       not to mention beaches unattended."
       "I get it", Henry resigned, before
       popping another awkward question.

"What only happened to blokes?"
"Fellers like you and me, you ask?
Oh, I see, it is not easy to answer,
to explain Henry, we have, well,
it is called political correctness.
men grimace an' bear the blight.

Dare open the mouth in protest
and they come gunning for you,

the thought Police. So, to kill the
boredom and time, we romance
idly about the footy all day long,
at least remaining left in peace."

If you believed Law was an ass
wait man, see what some By-laws
can do. Stop you building on stilts,
it is not their idea of modern styles,
flooding you out after heavy rains.

Should you catch a thief braking in
dare not raise a hand, why, the thief
taking your cattle and kids, same as
the crock are protected species, you
cannot take the Law into your hands; left
powerless and stumped, the Law is an ass.

Think of securing bushfire free zone
around your country abode. Think again
because the greenies will not let you do it.
Chop down a tree close to your home
they will sue you for what you are worth.
Go for a gun? Not allowed to have one.

Warts all and more was revealed
to Henry in one peak hour's train
journey on the Bankstown line,
carriage full, bodies overflowing
"Well, what about the Black Stump",
Henry was determined to find out.

"Salty paddocks many over-grazed.
'Faces in the Street', draft horses,
by motorcars and tractors updated.

Earners of your time, wool, hides
read the same outcome for tallow,
by iron ore, coal, minerals replaced,
big bikkies rolling in for the rich.

Poor there are no more begging
for a meal, Minimum Wage Award
changed a great deal. Bosses pay
us better; best's left for the Master.
Mind you, no real change there,
it is a heck of lot worse elsewhere.

City pubs betting shops now.
Shout or two, watch out Henry,
breathalyzer may get you too.
Just two middies and you hit
the limit of 0.5; anymore and
you should not drive that car.

Wattles, waratah you loved
still bloom after rain, we have
TV, Internet, media, cars and
jet planes, Oh, so busy we have,
none has got time for anyone.
The richer the more we want.

Old bark huts of Eurunderee.
early years of your childhood
eaten up by time and termites.
Squatters them's up and gone,
shot through for bright lights,
Not many's left on the land.

Fat Banks lord over empty

silent deserted outback tracks.
I know you have got a head full
Henry and who would not,
Just wait before you return
there to richly deserved rest.

  Given a choice Henry Lawson
  we have for you a simple test,
  1912 or 2021, where would you,
  we will leave this for very last,
  rather be? Or how about you
  be Australia Award nominee?"

SHE'LL BE RIGHT MATE

(A married Aussie couple touring Italy)

Thief! She yelled out loud, clutching
In vain after the snatched hand bag.
The scooter rider shot out of sight
Before you could blink an eye lid.
Harry took chase, blocked by crowd
Never got far. All for naught,
A few blocks away from Vatican.

Marge's soon crying, 'I was warned,
what a fool I am, now we are ruined.
Passports, air tickets, cards all gone,
Good Lord! Harry what are we to do?'
'Settle down Marge', he calmly replied,
The plane could well have crushed.
It could have been a whole lot worse.

He put his right arm around her,
'No worries she'll be right mate.'
They turned pockets inside out,
Looking for loose Euro change,
Then buzzed Harry's old man
Back on farm late in the arvo
Before he had knocked off to bed.

"Howyourgoin' dad, we are in Rome
Done like a dinner and stony broke."
"No worries me son, she'll be right."
So, it came back within seconds
Across the land and wide oceans. -

Now, there are fellers more refined
Much better qualified, but for grit
And chin up give me a country boy.

THE MEDITERRANEAN

Lavender, myrtle growing wild on karst cliff face
   next to the craggy black pine. Their scent's born on
     the wings of Mistral; tie me blindfolded and I will tell
       it could be nowhere else outside of Mediterranean.

     Med as the English like to call it, from island of
   Ithaca to Cyprus, Adriatic to Aegean, languages
change, banners and people; yet the same old Med.
     In tourist season there would be Northerners overflowing.

      But do come in the winter months when the bora
      gusts
        lash the coast; *caffeinon* is less than half full.
      When olives trees asleep shelter squawking gulls.
      When fishing boats denied strain on mooring ropes.
          there you can see the true Med.

     Drop in on a Sunday to the church, different faith,
      islanders will warm up to you, they do not mind
   Of history and heroes, let there be no mention
this time, nor would a thousand poems be enough.

MIND GAMES

How old never to age could one get
Presented with new eyes every day?
How fast could one run if never feet
Airborne had to touch solid ground.
And how rich would only one be, if for
every cent spent two fell from Heavens.
How, if, when and then, fill in the gaps.

If watch you can mindless destruction
and not be fuming or gun-ho incensed.
Or walk past a hungry child salivating
while munching on the sweet cake.
If observe crushing poverty you can
sing a song and pretend it is a mirage,
if, and when, how and then, fill in the gaps.

Why worry about this world on the backside
in palliative care on morphine, and how
can little me make any difference, and
Why do Heavens above condone atrocities?
Who am I to judge; sweet nothing to do with me,
just walk on steady there, look the other way.
If, and when, and then, just fill in the gaps.

One step forward, two steps backwards,
grass grows taller, some call that progress.
How come we are stuck in the same place?
One day at a time before you know
the sun rises where it did twelve months ago.
The same sun, place, the same time
just as warm and a year forever gone.

One on one is one, by one is one, carry
over, one into one is one, and only one.
If one, when and then, just fill in the gaps.

**Do this over and over again,
before your smile fades away.**

A NEW DAY

Who consumed darkness
and lit horizon on fire
at long last
fresh dew calls
on a rose bud
let us celebrate

Shadows shorten
ghosts timid no more
slide about
along the cold ground
a croaky rooster's wind pipe
plays a fuguette in F perhaps.

Once more and last, he tries
bellows his absolute best before
flock of galahs takes up
to challenge in display of
discordant crescendo and
shuts him up for good.
The cock will crow no more.

One with the earth tuned
in to feathery chorus tutti
not daring to speak
of new beginning
of Life's old theme
ancient theme
oldest of old.

Lo what is it I see next up high
a flock of Cape Barren geese in transit

formation, stunned I watch
unravel Nature's spectacle at work,
not daring to ask for more,
after all, who am I!

CONFUSED

A feline has nine lives people quote,
a man but one, yuck, a feline Master
only could have designed such like.
Hmm? What about canine, bovine and us?

On second reflections, wait,
Bible spoke of re-incarnation
maybe only as a demonstration,
Help please, has anyone come back?

What a fruitless deliberation
more than ever confused little me
after last night's nightmare.
Hang on, just wait to hear this:

In the year 1480 Knights Hospitallers
fend off Ottoman Turks
outnumbered 50 to 1, Crusaders last
foothold in Greece under siege
surrounded on Ionian island of Rhodes.

In the thick of the carnage
my sword is red, arms heavy
dead and wounded all around
in close man to man combat
busy dodging the buzdovan.

Lump of spiky iron on
short length of chain
widow maker par excellence
Turk new how to use well.
I ducked once I ducked twice.

Then gave as good as I got
only to run into a steel arrow
never knew had my name on it
pierce through my heart.
When woke up, I was dead.

Bathing in my own sweat.
Not so sure what to make of it
more and more confused.
Maybe someone can help.
Was this to be second coming?

I checked my arithmetic, how
can the second come before the first,
still shaking my bamboozled head,
busy pulling out the arrow
that pierced the heart.

NOBODY IS PERFECT

(Homage to Maxim Gorky)

Only with eyes of his
could eagle spot the miniscule
ant foraging on the ground.
Fully fed and content
eagle took pity on
the solitary little fellow.

'For goodness' sake, alone,
so small, such short sighted creature,
how can you ever find your way to
a morsel hidden on the ground?'

Ant scout heard the call and promptly replied.
You see, majestic Master of the sky that you
Little do you know there are cousins of mine
Hidden within you feathers flying unbeknown.

You see, big bird nobody knows it all.

PUSSYCAT

Silk purring on sofa
companionship of sorts
bricked inside city walls
pussycat and you
make for two.

Feline kind though
it must honestly
be said, will not
protect your life
nor guard your home.

Alert you of fire, nor
mourn at your grave site.
Folks do not mind
of superior hygiene
a pussycat groomed.

On show about house,
except when on heat
or when dropping
a litter of twelve
at the front door.

Fed on prime tit bits
primordial hunter instincts
bred out almost as graduate
mice and other sub-tenants
soon cotton on.

Kinds there are a few
Siamese, Cool, Tom cat

include more of the
two legged ones
smaller breeds too.

Half, quarter breeds
anything in between
they all mea-aw and pretend
to be your friend for a stroke
by loving hand and a feed.

LOVE II

Overused, abused, all encompassing
the most dangerous four letter word
use it sparingly if use you must,
for a lottery it is as much as anything.

> *You never know what you got*
> *until it is gone, and it is so.*
> *You never can tell how far to jump*
> *young man until you stumble and fall.*
> *You would be the last to know if*
> *that woman loves you in return.*

For words unspoken speak the loudest.
Silent glances exchanged read volumes
of burning nerves and bundle of desires,
time on triple fast and another scale.
Play hard and you will lose in the end,
play timid and you are not in the game.

> *Love can hurt you, lead not by the chin,*
> *and then again pretense is poor defense.*
> *Heart open and true plays game of love.*
> *If you can follow all that, miles ahead*
> *you are a winner in the lottery of love.*

THE SOUTH WIND

Talk to me
my old companion
of desires unfulfilled
of young days spent
in innocent games
you had been there
to watch it all
south wind.

Spirits of those
I loved
long gone
beyond horizon
you knew
of my despairs
face hidden
in the branches
of the olive tree.

Before you go
between
you and me
secret I can keep
that woman I gave
one and all for
how true was she?

Talk to me
of smiling
false hopes
wasted years

wasted lives
and stupid wars
you would have
seen it all
south wind.

TEREDO THE WORM

Was it Archimedes the Greek
who made the iron float
news to a nasty customer
Teredo the Worm.

Sweet timber set out to sea,
huon pine, oak and teak,
yummy morsels for voracious
Teredo the Worm.

Tempest, seducing Sirens, and
rocks growing at sea all a dread
to Mariners, none to eat the ship
from under you but, Teredo the Worm.

He would chew hidden from view
nibble day and night without sound
curse upon the sea faring folks
Teredo the Worm.

At last, hurrah, hurrah for Archimedes
ahoy, we are afloat safe as house
guess who needs new dentures, none other
then Teredo Navalis the Worm.

MACHINE AGE

Men, coolies, machine, robots.
All but robots turfed out since, gone,
down to robots only 24/7,
in a happy ¾ little tune sang in chorus:
clink, clonk, clank -clink, clonk, clank.

Robot army end to end
sign on to join their brethren
without penalty rates and
sick leave nonsense in the way.
What is to be done with workers?

Robots win men lose every time,
it is no brainer, and no more pay.
$$$ rain from Heavens, not
 for them production line workers
blue collar and white.

In the long run masses bankrupt
cannot buy what factories churn out.
Pollies and banksters of the day
must know the answer to that, like
we are all history in the long run.

Until then watch hydraulic arms
flailing about singing a nursery tune:
clink, clonk, clank, -clink, clonk, clank,
'cause all of them happy robots needs are
 Volts AC, pushbutton and a grease can.

LAZY RIVER

This new religion portals we have
Internet it is called, at heart surely,
children of Ma' Nature's we remain.
If anything drives home the truth
lazy rolling river does it eating time.
So why am I telling you all this?

> Worn out my fellow man before
> expiry date? Suicidal, broke, maybe
> driven bonkers by jittery economy?
> Do yourself a favor, snap out,
> camp along a lazy river for a week,
> just leave 'must have' toys behind.

It beats psychiatrists' ends up.
GPs in the country they know,
if only therapeutic value
was to be duly gazetted.
Alas, it is unlikely to happen
any time soon my fellow man.

> Should you still have it in you to
> follow this route, take a fishing rod
> a pair of binoc's and a frying pan.
> Little else apart from a tent, air bed
> a box of matches and an LPG bottle.
> Real life you will meet, not virtual,
> like

fish jump, herons stalk and whirls form,
as nothing runs forever in a straight line,
least of all a lazy river. Them river folks
and fauna live a good life for most part,
relaxed about Internet fraud, carry on
Facebook, margins, and ticking deadlines.

WORK SHY

sleepy head through the night
long dark night in slumber
dark long night all alone
a dream I had born of slumber

first sunlight pretended
to offer company to offer work
more likely to offer
company of toil no end

oh sweet dream born of slumber
with me born in the black night
born in the long black night,
come back for company

come back my sweet dream
born of slumber in a black night
new dawn has company I hear
task upon a task from dawn to dusk

ROMANCE II

More than sum
Of individual parts
A synergy of sorts
Is a couple in love.
An economist
In love with sums
Would put it like that

Hear a psychologist next
Maddening idiosyncrasies
Of the partner or a spouse
When all taken in stride
Closed one or both eyes
Blind as a bat I sniff that
Irrationality points to **l o v e**

Joe Blow's turn next
When for the first time
In front of the mirror
You rehearse the lines
Find shoes unpolished
Discard a dozen shirts
And settle on a jacket
odds on a safe bet it looks
Love is there to claim you
About to scramble the brains

Lastly GP's insomnia diagnosis
When sleep is hard to come by
Blood pressure reads whoops (!)

There is too many a chore
Long overdue, that should
Have been done yesteryear
Poor man you have problems
Cupid has picked you off on
Cloud nine without a parashoot

**Now have some Diazepam pills
To settle your Dopamine down**

MAN, VS CHIMP TRIBAL LORE

Lowly soldier, or highly general
bullet carries no name, except,
no slug kissed a highly general
since Crusades, nor has died in battle
a King since Gustav the Great.

When lauded powers of reason
head for the door we have wars.
Hairy jungle cousins unlike us
they kill to eat, to defend the turf,
they also know when to call stop.

And then, the gap between the best
some of us can dish out against the
abominable worst is getting worse
than animals' we hypocrites dare
call wild, worse than chimpanzees.

And then why are those rolling in loot
adverse to share, to comply with
taxation rules, instead they scrounge on
paying a fare wage? Us oh, so smart,
let fools halfwits end up paying tax.

And lastly, why are power hungry creepy
chameleons allowed to thrive, no matter
which —ISM wind blows; two of a kind,
in cohorts with Mafia bosses seated
in the front pew? Why? Folks want to know.

In age of humbug, empty word gold plated
since regurgitated to mere pretense, power

of white lie, even the knights' chivalry
of the Middle Age has been debauched.
It's cool *bab'* there *ain't* no dirty money.

I score chimp ahead on most counts,
shame on poor second-best the man-tribe.
All the lawyers hired guns, nor media
circus and admen a legion, nor them
moguls make a scrap of difference,
born is a new species of invertebrate.

LOVE III

194

would I ever go   *to share with you*
would I go with you   *to share*
would I ever   *what is there*
to Earth's end go   *with you*
just you and me   *eyes, I would*
you want to know   *for love only*

GEMINI

Of twin sisters
hard to tell apart,
frugality is shade
prettier than poverty,
this few can deny.
While love and sex
no Gemini these two,
lumped into one
is a common mistake.

Glorious youth
exuberance and myth,
if only it would last.
Why does one
need first to mature
where blood flow
begins to slow
only then to recognize
nature's practical joke
male's sexual peak
at the age of sixteen!

An albatross pair
mates for life,
measured in
many long years.
Over in seconds
is their coitus act.
Clearly love
not sex is the mortar
and cement that binds,
 media admen got this one
back to front all wrong.

NATURE'S JOKER

You just meat in the way
static electricity charged,
the hair shoots up, eye pupils go wide,
there(!), a pair of large emerald eyes
glow menacingly in the dark.
On high zoom size it may look in order,
spooky to unaided eye. What is there?
Ach, just Nature's joke, wall mounted glass.
      Once in a leap year the bird,
      a lone bird pays a visit here,
      snow white Artic pigeon
      in sub-tropics out of place.
      Inquisitive bird spends hours
      looking for whom or what?...
Bedroom door goes shut,
none is anywhere near it
and there is no draft.
Squeaky hinges in code pass
message to the Grim Reaper
invisible somewhere close, us fools
scared to the bone; worried
about Nature's idea of acting funny.
      A message is received
      never sent, nowhere near
      a courier or semaphore
      neither mushrooms, LSD,
      nor radio waves in play,
      so what Nature's joke is this
      that finds one in disbelief!...
Youth of sixteen green as chlorophyll,
apex of his sexual drive curve
it is downhill from hereon, he

holds testosterone loaded gun of
wishful dreams, by any other
measure clearly still immature,
worse still, underage and broke.
Oh, what a dumb waste this is!
Worst kind of Nature's joke, except:
> Of six wives Henry the VIII condemned
> 'cause none bore him a Tudor prince,
> not one Ladyship the Queen was guilty
> as charged, all fault of syphilitic Henry.,

STEADY AS SHE GOES

Late still in bed every minute becomes precious
That cup of coffee a tad too hot you gulp down
Running for the exit door. No time to day-dream
Car engine jumps to life, we take off in second gear.

Turn the first corner, the motor still running on choke
And gulping petrol, whoops that light just went red.
Hard on the brake pedal and her nose goes down.
Tires squealing that P plater behind is on high beam.

Winter nights are long and street lights still on at 6AM.
You wait and wait it is a bad intersection, and there is
That petrol head in the fast lane, wroom wroom wroom
Riding the clutch. It gets to one, should I burn off the moron?

Do not lose your cool old-timer; you ought to know better,
Like Guardian angel that red light camera watches over you.
Relief at last we motor to the next set of traffic lights.
Who only is that Daimler Benz in the Bus Lane?

Tales of commuter daily grind would fill many a poem
And novel at least one, on another note once on open road
Do not be a fool and go for the gas pedal. For many are
Travails of the commuter, red light and speed cameras
just two.

Law obeying you just motor on, steady as she goes,
You will get there if takes all day and another day to return.
Let those hot heads pass you on the inside, they will not
for long,
Heard of unmarked Police cars? Just motor on steady as
she goes.

ALICE SPRING REGATTA

Unlucky to freeze
In Moscow zoo whilst
It is dawn and already
warmish thirty two
In shade at Alice Spring
Where a mob of red 'roos
Moscow zoo cousins
Here in the suburbia
Graze the night through

On Todd's River dry bed
A regatta is to take place
A real regatta we are told
On real NT river sand
A true sensation
World's one and only
Regatta on sand
Media and tourists
Swoop down on Alice
Adorned in her finest

Life begins to stir at Alice
At first daylight
A Police van pulls up
To pick up strugglers
After a hard night's binge
Log fires to be put out
In city parks hence
Free ride assured
Back to humpies
At the outback station

Rubbish collection truck

Calls up next to gather
Bedding of sorts and
Litter empty booze
Containers for most part
Police leave cancelled
Let the regatta begin
Cheers and salute to all
Part takers and spectators
Of many different
Cities and nations
Skipper and deckies
Brave seamen all

Ahoy ten minutes
To the starting gun
And countdown
Helmsman maneuver
The craft on reach
Watch out starboard
For pushy upstarts

Starter's gun off
Hell for leather
From hereon
It is free for all
Downwind we run
No handicap rating
Either sailing in NT
On spinnaker leg
Downwind we run
As one in quick step

To the finishing line
Downwind we run
Without a spinnaker

Blooper or big genny
By our own feet we run
To the finishing line
Received in jubilation
By many already on turps
In heat and cloud of dust
Here in Alice Springs NT

DIRTY MONEY

Carol is a fine ol' girl
O fine ol' girl is Carol
Carol is a good ol' girl
Sing in chorus all of us
Oodles of money to burn
And heaps more to come

Carol is a fine tipster
To cabbies and waiters
Like some rich Princes
Carol is a fine ol 'dame
So, let us drink no shame
Champaign to that
On Carol's expense

Carol thinks
Money is sin,
'cause the fortune
She inherited
Used to be
House of ill repute
Whorehouse and
Gambling den
Two in one
Service station

Carol is a class act
If sins of the past
Can be redeemed
She is on her way
Good on Carol
Last cent evaporated

I hope the big Papa
In Heavens above
Looks after Carol
No one else will.

COUNTRY AIR

(MOLTO VIVACE)

'No, no, no and no,
Wealthy squire,
Thanks, but your bride
Sire, I shall never be!
Not for all the gold
Shall I be told
Of me riches none,
Potato farm Ma an' Pa,
Nor of me six long years
Grind in Primary class.

Defeated wealthy Jack
Used to have his way:
'How so bonny Louise,
My money is of no use?'
'Sire speaks of money and gold
Poor me of lasting love to behold.
My own true love
Will stand by me
In want and poverty.'

Months went by,
Louise with child,
And true love at HM's
Given long stretch
In Long Bay behind bars,
Spoiled four eyes Jack
On news arrives back.

With a fresh proposal.

He would have given
Of hectares half a glen
And Angus half a herd,
To jump in bed naked
With luscious Louise.

'Oh, what a delight good Sire
To have you back, yes of course Jack,
White wedding you says
To take place, Where? When?
On the 'morrow in de kirk?!
Wow, that is some quick!

Ach silly lassie me,
Forget about the past,
Now that you do ask,
Given to childish rant
All in jest of course.
Here all that you see Sire,
Fair game of your desire.

There is Jack ere I *forgets*
One thing I must confess,
Passions will have to
Endure bide a wee,
'cause I've got me days.' -
A white lie no matter,
Hooray, all for Louise.
A message to moneybags:

**'Money buys land, goods,
An' services, not honesty.'**

A MERE MALE

Bright sun at noon shone overhead
 under the shadow of a wild fig tree.
'I love you', she whispered, the sweet thing,
 young niece all of six years
tugging at my shirt sleeve.

Elated over the Moon was I till,
next day clouds gathered overhead.
As it began to rain,
'I love you not', she said.
Left speechless I looked back.

 Is it my beard fifty micron longer,
an ice cream denied,
 or fickle nature of love?
A mere male the odds are,
I will never get to the bottom of this.

DNA IS BUT A BRICK

An elephant can never
Bite a tick up the bum
To return the favor.
Acquired wisdom tells us
There was not a green frog yet
Suicidal enough to bite a snake.

The old order tossed overboard
All the hype is about the DNA.
DNA this and DNA that.
It may as well stand for
Do not ask how Chimp and Man
Can be 98 percent of the same?

No Chimp ever wrote
A commercial ditty,
That I know of.
Never mind a symphony,
Nor wrote a book or paid tax.
DNA's a building brick.

A palace or a hovel,
A brick goes into either.
Up the Master Builder to decide
Who is the biter and who the *bitee*.
DNA in complex life looks like
Just another building brick.

CON LA NOSTALGIA

(To memory of Miguel Hernandez)

From afar I hear foreign voices call my name.
Up closer human feet forest tramples the earth,
Ever more feet, ever more exposed curvy flesh.
Humanity tides surge in and out twice a day
None left cold. Not on the outside anyway.
Summer is back in Costa del Sol, Spain, 2012.

The orange-red ball never tired shines
democracy for all, true for black, small,
rich and tall; man, or beast, no difference.
It shines free in equal measure for young and old.
Towards evening last human tide washes ashore,
While red roofs stretch out long shadows in the East.

Sea breeze sweeper oleander scented toils for free.
Tall antennas now busy pierce the blue sky in the eye.
Night cloak descends and stars multiply by the hour.
Street lamps like infantry men as one jump to attention.
Cycle of life continues monarchy or republic, once again
Wretched poor retire to the smoky tin shed hovel fire.

Light that escapes from windows above though,
Upon the cobble stone street below is cold as ice.
It knows not of long naked years wrapped in hunger.
Nor of dames who left perfume on Miguel's foreskin.
It will never shine over poems scribbled on prison walls,
Nor touch poet widow's misery folded inside black poncho.

Nearby Flamenco guitar chords join in the nocturne.
Melancholy images cascade, then float up my room.
The sadness stays with me and the sorrow remains.
Images of Miguel Hernandez full of life before the war
Took his manhood and let him die in jail come to life.
Miguel and legions of the best and for whom or for what!

FROM ORPHAN BOY TO A MAN
(AUST.)

Like wild flower unattended along the road side
an orphan grows into adulthood on sufferance.
Silent hours into silent days into silent years
eyes spent now dry to give have no more tears.

Angelic hand in empathy may appear
only to continue benevolent journey
down the road to somewhere else in more need.
Hence, back to noisy dormitory battlefield.

Orphaned boy grows street wise. To each his own.
He has none to claim, instead plays what is in it for me,
scratch my back and I will scratch yours, no time to
play infantile games, life here follows Rafferty rules.

Orphaned girl marries early as a rule
to escape drudgery of kitchen maid for life
or a whole lot worse. Boy grows into
a solitary man scarred by fights and abuse.

It is only when the good ol 'Army calls
the orphaned youth is first in queue line.
Pay is good and you will have mates,
the Army to stand by you if not a family.

Backbone of high tensile steel, gaze of an eagle,
spring in the marching step, wearing a slouch hat,
his country's symbol, here is the orphaned boy
made into a fine young man wearing AIF uniform.

JUDGMENT DAY

Night skyline flickers ruby red tongues of fire.
Moonshine crystals of night before lying around
Shattered in pieces, while stokers of Hades toil.
Escape there is none from here,
      This is the end of the line.

Wretches for something to do
Shuffle the feet as the names
Go up in Heavenly lights.
Judgment Day is here, for them
      All roads lead to Hell.

Lord's Triumvirate rules supreme:
Bloodsuckers and murderers
Prostrate beg for pardon in vain.
More broken cogs on the junk pile
      Of the doomed humanoid machine.

Enter hyena lane, vultures next to pick the bones.
Of what's left fired cauldron will kill the stench.
Out of the crucible ashes a new breed is to rise.
In a new future, free of masters and slaves.
      Where all life is sacred a more human mankind.

POEM OF THE COMMON MAN

What is a poem ordinary folks ask?
Expert scribes adamant they know,
righteous to deny what is not
up to their pre-conceived meters.
What poetry is forms a debate.
It should be the reader to decide,
or else we may never agree.

A blade of grass in the breeze
searching for quantum of
UV light it needs to grow.
A beehive buzzing with flights
arrivals and departures.
Snowflakes blocking the horizon
on a winter day. Does any qualify
if not abstract enough?

Perhaps a dejected lover
suicidal in despair.
A death of one close,
a ballad of a broken heart?
Does the poetry end
with last tear drop shed.
When do you tell a muse:
'it's stepmother Grammar's turn?'

Until a dawn some day when many
will wake up as one of heart, for mine
row poetry is in every living thing
as it breaths to leave behind
footprint in sand, or ripples on water.
It is there for anyone attuned

with open eyes to observe
in contours of the land,
beauty of oceans and hills beyond.

In every living thing,
lovers' embrace,
flutter of butterfly wings,
inspired bird song,
rumble from the war front
rhyme rhythm and refrain,
I find in all of them,
poetry of a common man.

EASY DOES IT

Mangrove swamp end to end,
Till one sunny day
Hocus pocus, a
Residential building block.
At the stroke of a pen
Easy does it my friend.

> From a Biblical Noah's flood
> To unwelcome water intrusion
> No liability of course,
> Says Insurance Co Ltd;
> At the stroke of a pen,
> Easy does it again.

'Men all equal before Law',
Broke, you think what a joke.
Take care before at the stroke of the pen
You find yourself in calaboose.
Mortal public enemy number one
To a thriving democracy.
Black's white an' white is black,

> Repeat it a hundred times like the
> Media
> Until I bet you see a zebra ahead. Or
> try
> "Men and women are equal",
> Well on the way to turn
> Into hermaphrodites.

Still, push your pen all your like.
White shall never taint black paint.
Men can never have children while women
Fight not to Lord Queensbury rules,
But pull hairs, scream insults and punch below belt.
Unlike men, who fight just because it is in the testis.

Women fight for keeps.
 No more easy does it!
And then, "Illegal merchandise"
To you, not so, just try to make
Some Customs look the other way.
Carry on; pen is mightier than sword,

Mightier still is the lubrication everyone knows,
And pretense, just going through the motions.
Do not upset the rich and mighty, rather
End up joining other bipedal invertebrates.
Be damned if society really, really cares,
Well on a one way joy ride to Hell.

COSSACK BALLAD

Sing for me before I depart for good
Of barehanded men fighting off
Hungry wolves howling in deep snow!
My gravely worn out old baritone
Frightens baby and stampedes horse.

Dance for me *kozachok* to *bandura* playing,
I would, except my knee is sure to spring!
Mount that black stallion, wild as the steppe
Without a saddle! I would do it again except,
Broken ribs refuse to heal an' hurt like hell,
While breath is harder and harder to inhale.

Chase the skirt for me Yevgeny, as I used to once!
Last time I tried *zhensky* laughed; called it a joke.
All this 'n more pain is sure to come your way
Without asking should you be around as long as I.
Till then, if in need of help, or fatherly advice?
Young *efraiter* report here to your Commander.

Mind you not before time, so do make haste! -
How to shoot straight, make every bullet count.
How to fight in battle, trust but *Bog* Almighty.
Die not like betrayed Stenka Razin in chains?
You can learn it all here, from your dying *ataman*.

INTEMEZZO

(OUTSOURCED)

Temperature shot from frost
To jungle like steaming hot as
She wore a wide brimmed hat,
Not a stitch apart from that.

Wrapped in body pheromones
A raptor closed in on a timid man.
Grammar slayer soprano of hers
Packed atmospheric turbulence.

Explicit enough to raise the dead:
Ready, set, horny, charge again!
So be it! Defeated and captured,
Paper defense collapsed in a heap.

A cyclone bore down on him,
A cyclone named Josephine.
Devastation it left behind
To be on her pretty head.

Whereto does a cyclone retire
Devastation over; there,
Pretty head Josephine's
Must be also her lair.

She left perfume on foreskin
With some pubic hair, then
Tip-toed into the dark night.
O, what a Birthday present!

A wide brimmed hat he recalls, that sat
On a pretty head, and that was that.
She stole the peace, now gone,
Old bones curse the frost return.

BOY SOLDIER

Oversize tin hat wobbles from side to side
with every movement the boy makes.
But do not be deceived, snigger not just yet,
that grenade launcher slung over the shoulder
touching the ground is a serious weapon of war.

His cousin's, six year old tiny fingers fondle
A Kalashnikov mistaken for a Teddy Bear.
But wait, do not snigger just yet, those digits
ready to sever undefended limb have killed before,
around the blood red fields of Africa and Middle East.

Other than arms merchants does anyone really, really care?
Can UN feed kids thrown to dogs of war now and forever?
Those who never were kids, and what about the time before,
when roads were not pot holes; work for all, Law and Order
prevailed? Hey, you ostriches, yes, once upon a time...........!

ALL CLERKS NOW

A retiree returns to his native land
Three generations later.
In his imaginational vivid picture:
A line of giant she oaks centuries old,
Lush meadows and a crystal clear brook
Teeming with game to mark the boundary,
Stocked with brown trout and bass.

With children on the way to school, along the banks
He would pick crocus, snowbells and violets
After winter snow and catch a trout or two.
Timber mills ate the oak. Men squander the loot.
Thorny acacia planted for something
To hold the soil, here still out of place
Droop homesick for Africa. You look for
Lush pastures, no hoof and no paw there.

End to end just overgrown scrubby mess.
Where a brook used to run; water we drank
Dead cats float, Death is in command.
Dirty foam bubbles on the canal,
The air is hydrogen sulfide.

Downcast crushed in defeat
I return to the village to meet.
All clerks these days bemoaning loudly
Again, and again, there is no work
And no money to be had.
While, more squealing piglets than teats I do see.
Penned saw running out of milk that will not eat.

Hawks cannot get at factory chicken,

Ground's empty of hoof and paw.
But there(!), vultures stalk
Feathers ruffled, beaks at the ready
Measuring each other for bones to pick.
If myopic Man would pause to read Nature's signs
Before money, or each other is all that is left to eat.

C282

From Bridgewater to Malden
In Garden State of Vic
Relax (!) driving is easy
On the eye, why, C282 she is
Another well maintained
And tar sealed rural road.

Until you reach what is left
Of that ironbark gum tree
Broken trunk and charred bark.
At the foot of it in Memoriam
Of Johno under sign of cross
A faded garland.

Pain his second name,
Heartbreak to those
Who cared for the brat.
Their silver inscription reads:
'RIP Johno, your mates
Under eighteen Magpies.'

At 2 AM Johno did a runner
High on dope and red P plate
Into a dog leg at full bore.
Stolen V8 Airborne
Old man gum tree
The final stop.

At seventeen young years
No longer a lad
Not yet a man
Yet old enough to
Bruise hearts of many
Who once cared.

Given fewer gangster movies on offer

Who can tell if John was to reform?
After distressed Amboes chocking let
us hope
Other cats do not foolishly copy His
finale to blazing inferno.

GERIATRIC LAMENT

To impatient young ones who cannot wait
For oldies to move first foot under
Or to over-dose, wait!

Dreams of property you never raised a sweat for
It may or not come your way
Just hang on there!

And if any self-esteem you have left
Would you want it
Any other way?

For yesteryear's Heroes in their eighties
Black and white faded picture they see is
All they still have in a memory and in 2D.

Merriment vibrato of years ago silenced.
Voices of what once ruled the airwaves
But minor key discords floating in space.

NO MORE TEARS TO SHED

Long Northern winter spent
Spring time returned, it should be
Time to rejoice but it is not.

Skies of pewter forebode a storm to
A lone pine tree where a forest used to grow
Pleading to Heavens above for sulfur free air.

What took a Century to grow, housed
Birds and song, chain saw men felled
In a single day for a handful of dollars.

Back from Tropics a lonely stork hen circles
All morning over a demolished wheat silo
Where a pair raised chicks only last Autumn.

One tree, one bird destined to die out, limit to
Desolation and hot sterile tarmacs there is none,
Step in step with modern man's machines.

Burden of never enough Man carries within
His crooked DNA to the end of the line
All the way to the gates of Hades.

More animal species are doomed to extinction,
Without Future, and who wants to care
When dirty or not money is all that shines?

Dry eyes of mine have no more tears to shed.
Fishes, birds and all living creatures condemned
To oblivion, when you do cry, cry for me too.

FROM MANDY TO ANDY IN ACTS THREE

Act 1.

Wine waiter Miguel practicing pidgin French
pirouettes around mahogany table
decked for two with porcelain and silver ware.
Under crystal chandeliers dispersed bundles of
bright photons make for Hilton night splendor,
and sweet romance is percolating in the air.
To freshman Mark six *foot* five Footy star all of this,
Crimean caviar entree, Meum champers
and five course meal when one would do only
over-indulgence to be sweated off under *physio*.
Not to mention her sweet words of passion
'Hey *Darl*' give your wallet a rest tonight!

Act 2.

Inside the apartment she dims the lights
and she dims it some more
Mark there wandering why
It takes so long to peel off clothes.
Luxurious wig falls off on the floor as
Mandy metamorphoses into Andy.
Long eye lashes, manicured toe nails
Dior perfume and golden necklace
all for dross, now with a black eye.
Like a flash Mark jumps out of bed,
from horny to placid in a millisecond.
Clothes collected under arm stark naked
panic stricken charging for the fire escape.

Act 3.

At nightshift portiere Sam's desk, a drama scene unfolds.
Sam good at First Aid had seen all of this play out before.
'Yes Sir, oops, Maam your eye is OK, let me fetch the Rollce
valet is due back in a *jiffy.*'She, oops he sighs in tears:
'No thank you *sport*, I'll rather take the cab home.
What a horrible night wasted on a hired *limo* and that
 agro comedian country bumpkin Footy forward!- - -
Now wait there a tick Sam, what did I do with *me bra*?'

THE WORLD SHRUNK AND GOT UGLIER

In Memoriam of Claudio Abbado (1933 – 2014)

Hard task master
on a false note, yet
never abusive to
an under-performer.
Bestowed upon
every Medal of Honor,
Doctorates a page full yet
never seen showing off one,
Maestro Claudio Abbado
or CA to young musicians
fortunate enough to play under
a life time dream come true.
A conductor like no other.

Retired in poor health
CA still conducted
without score
almost to his dyeing breath.
Money and fame par for the course
mattered little to the Milanese
the most beautiful mind of my time.
Just think of Venezuelan street kids
Maestro took under wing
pro Bono and nurtured to
South America's best Youth Orchestra. - - -

Since your passing Claudio Abbado
for music lovers and poets
the Universe shrunk
and the world got a whole lot uglier.

STANDING LIKE A LONELY TREE

130 Decibels at low KHz register
low enough to shake brick walls
teens and boppers dare call music.

Through cloud of pot smoke
one's attention focuses on tattoos
grotesque enough to scar for life.

Rings through nose and pendants
looking down condescending they
chose to call it the generation gap.

Drugged to the eyeballs full of
silly old man, look poor oldies
forced to accept their new norm.

Euphoria intoxicated, mundane
Long ago substance obliterated
street-wise oldies left but aghast.

Forced to observe you impotent
broken down buttress younger by day
victims preyed on by drug dealers.

Like wild goats salivating on clover
green saplings shooting all around.

BORN REBELS

AFTER EUGENE DELACROIX

Think (!), …. if agitated mob hollered:
"Guilty, guilty, burn the evil witch!",
Could you be swayed condoning the wrong?…
.

Assume a brilliant scientist made
Our Sun to shine ad infinitum
At a benign angle of incidence.

Winter and dark night abolished,
Would all necessarily agree?
Maybe, accent being on not.

For there is an indefinable odd ball gene
Within some rebels whose spine comes
To world of much higher tensile strength.

Who question rather than concur, who
At high cost rebuke perfumed rubbish
Self-interested barons loudly proclaim.

With toll rising few of them remain still
Left in our midst, once a thorn in the eye
To *toffs* 'born to rule and pay no tax'.

Methods change, targets remain,
Dispatched from willing henchmen,
Dungeons, dispossession and terror.

Leave out not media spin willing
Batteries of mercenary QC lawyers,

Trumps cards in a court amphitheater.

But for the rebels there would be
No *Republique r*efuge for common men.
In its place to prevail inbred Royal pantomime.

Comic graces and top hats
To lord over plebs
Shackled till the end of time.

Red not blue blood
Spilt in too many places,
Bastille barricades just for one.

Like Guy Fawkes' kin
Subjected to Merciless retribution,
Iron lungs and claymore blade.

Yet no matter how
Horrendous the punishment,
Call for Freedom or Death of 1848,

It is sure to be heard again by and again by,
Men born rebels, t appears clear to all,
No substance changed in the interim.

ATTILA FOREVER

On the front line
Limbs and grenades
Fall from the sky
Men shiver to the bone
Even on a hot day

In a blizzard of ash
Civilization reduced
To a fancy word
Sun ceased shining
Attila is back or has he
Never left this place

Grass a hardy weed may yet
Grow back in years natured
On the blood of nameless fallen
And sadly, Man has yet to accept
Maxim other than my tribe amen

Win at all costs orders come from HQ
Bomb the UN Schools and
MSF Hospitals to be sure but
Fear not it is losers rather than winners to
Front up before the War Crimes Tribunal

MOTHER EARTH GIA

Of crystal clear brook's water
I had my fill in younger days and
Ladies who shared my smile
I did look them up in the eye.

On long voyages my sailing boat's keel
Autographed the Ocean if for an instant.
Of Sibelius and Mendelssohn, I have heard and
Admired Michelangelo, Rodin and Mestrovic. - - -

And now you ask and ask me again trivia.
Time and time all over again you want to know
If Life is no more than Russian roulette and
If I am broke or guilty of playing games?

What is true and what false, who is fit to tell?
Me and you and the whole lot of us free-loading
To Gia Mother Earth could not be less important.
Mere cancer cells intruders trespassing.

So, hear me now woman and hear me good
When games I play use a ball not people,
And Russian roulette short I drew
On the very day I was born.

Back to true or false, one or the other
Which one of the two suits you better?
Altogether a very subjective matter,
Resigned I give up on that one.

Of more importance to know should be:
Once the last Native beyond the horizon
Who will be left there to care and cry to
Mother Earth for devastation we caused?

RETAIL INVESTOR'S BALLAD

Mug punter Mr. Brave Foolhardy
Cash in your fortunes before you step into
A stock market boxing ring
To slug it out with Super heavy-weights

Computer algorithms and funny sales
Threaten to floor you TKO in round one
And if somehow you manage to escape clinches
Of growling bears punching under belt and shorting

Celebrate not nor drop mouth guard just yet
For an uppercut by Chinese buggy buggy man
Is a gonna git yu before the bell of this be certain
Then drive your share price right where it hurts most.

ADVANCE AUSTRALIA FAIR

Prospecting pre-Cambrian outcrops
We endure 40 degrees plus under
Shade of an old ghost gum tree
Towering over bush and spinifex.

Starved of oxygen struggling for breath
Ngaru my guide sums it up matter of fact:
'Him white fellow Gubbo no belong here.
Soft skin stranger and rocks don't match'.

Unlike those born under star-dome
Who way back in the Dream Time
Walked barefoot quietly attuned to
Great Serpent and power of Wandjina.

Rugged over-cooked land owned them
They did belong no question, discount him
No belong whitey and Ngaru tribal elder
No longer, like a whitey discard him as well.

A knot of sun baked dust coated streets
Asleep under scorching sun is Marble Bar,
Where men black, white and in between
Day dream and chase flies all day long.

Others, men and women a few gather
Inside the only pub chilled to the bone
By polar icy whirlwind overhead idly
Blessed chattering away the calendar.

Yes, I know and you know Dreaming over

And done it is my shout black mate. As for
Advance Australia fair? To clear the air
Tell us Ngaru who belongs and where!

BACK TO LIFE FROM

THE DARK SIDE

To Donovan

When short of nutrients and water
required to keep one fit and sane
just a single glimpse into darkness
is more like invitation to a dream.

Or when the Sun shines low if at all
and turns off nav' lights to the soul
Stairway to Heavens once nearby,
why then hands clutch into empty air?

On the side of endless time and space
rests dark energy silent to all but those
who had been there if only in a dream
yet harmonious with our Cosmos vibes.

Doped on sweet Love or toxic on Hate,
push or shove in darkness matters none.
Differentials first and second equal zero
and all accounts are permanently closed.

Left for cold hands to grip colder steel
hitching a ride, and may Gods bless your
Gnostic souls there boldly queue jumping
a ride on Stairway to Heavens' elevator.

Escaping the morass where money is
the damn thing that shines, and the sin

is to get caught red handed in the midst
of wrong committed upon more wrong.

In darkness our footing's insecure until
a bolt of lightning reveals a dismal scene,
cold hands many more one over the other
in mad clamor for Pearly Gates domicile.

Long nightmare finally drawing to end
morning sun old friend's back smiling,
fresh due settles down on a rose bud
life and light are back let us celebrate

PARADISE O'STRA'IA

Bacchus fermented grapes for the plebs,
them aristocrats et al to indulge in wine, only
to stagger around fog brained, reminiscing
what might have been 'if only ', or next best,
to smudge nagging gut pains in the process. - - -

Sparta's King Leonidas,
valiantly fought and died
Invading Persian hordes.
Greeks free but what an act,
Athenians never said thanks. - - -

And Frederick Chopin bed ridden
on lung TB wrote nostalgic Nocturnes that
have me love sick with scattered thoughts
judging my fellow men; stiff arthritic fingers
struggling in vain over cords black and white. - - -

All said, thanks a million times
to this free land terra Australis.
Never mind idle dreamers
busy searching for Nirvana
Paradise in another dimension? - - -

Ask those who had been
to Hell and back again.
No reminder needed of
a knock on the door at 2 AM.
Paradise Oustraia is right here.

For diligent ones at least
having taken to the sun baked

red soil, its lonely long roads.
To its wild ocean shores,
calling it their own.

ROBOTS IN TANKA

Men and slave robot once
All but robot turfed out since, gone
Down to robots 24/7
Sing in chorus nursery tune
Click clock clack grrr click clock clack.

Robots' army end to end
Sign to join their able brethren
Wages do not come in.
Of sick leave nonsense let there
Never be a word of mention.

Robots beat men "Masters"
It is no brainer and no pay.
$$$ rain from heavens
Not for them production workers
Laid off blue collar and white.

Masses stony broke
Cannot buy what robots churn out;
Pollies of the day
Must have answers to that, like
In the long run we are all dead.

Until then watch robot arms
Flailing about to a nursery tune
Click grrrr clack grrrr clack,
'cause them happy robots need is
but 240 Volts AC and a grease can.

GHOSTS OF OZ BLACK AND WHITE

(1) Caked red earth
clumps of weed
not a blade of grass
 as far as one can see
not a ray of hope

(2) Dry river bed pebbles
glitter in sunlight, false hope
littered with old boots leans
broken down river fence

Steel posts do not rust here
the air is too dry their cousins
timber posts sand blasted
expose grains polished smooth

Sky raiders raven undertakers
stubbornly defy natural selection
pitch black distressed they remain
soaking up the scorching sun

While screeching lament they emit
chills one to the bone
requiem no doubt for some
horrible offender from distant past

Of machines works of Man
only 4x4 tire tracks remain
momentarily exposed soon
to be erased in shifting dunes and then
From world away in the Big Smoke
Banksters demand

squeeze water out of sand
grow thirsty cotton

On and no end we see fruits of
profit driven delusion rather
reject the hand of reason
let it all crumble to dust

So, we the bunnies
can in the future
cometh the bitter end
chew on the banknotes

      A prospector a tourist a bum
         one cannot but feel empathy
         for battlers who eked out a living
      here largely ignorant and died broke

      Caked red Oz earth.
         mile upon a mile
         not a blade of grass
      that one can see
         not a ray of hope you would think yet

      Do I see what others have missed;
         a dreamer to come along to this land
      refunded as barren to Mother Earth
         where a newcomer I find peace of mind
      and Ghosts of Oz black and white

Caked red Oz earth
from the Black stump to off the map
Not a ray of hope you would think
dare to look in the future though you are free
and have never been more wrong

LAND OF FALSE SMILES

Registration time on Earth lapsed
strain to depart with a broad smile.
Leave over-crowded world behind
with a broad smile on your face,
even on fire hurting like Hell.

Smile if it is the last thing you do
basking in the land of the Big Smile
Facebook, Tweeter and Instagram.
No matter if just robbed blind
or if a bus ran over both leg.

Grimace from ear to ear expose
false dentures no matter, it is in vogue
just as you wonder why everything is
priced at ninety-nine; and why
them Pollies drive us all psycho.

For last, here and why only
 a few have stashed monies
while most roll small change
in shallow leaky pockets
and hungry street kids suck

on the thumb for taste of something,

SILENCE

Alone at four AM I walk
the streets of a giant spider web
City they call it
Streets resting paved with silence
wrapped in outflow scent

For transient company try neutrinos
they travel through you and
mindlessly on through space
just like the thoughts
of a lonely walker before dawn

For one, if only new born were
destined to a higher purpose away
from the economical meat grinder
After all Man lived for Millennia
Stat's free only to become ensnared

Under cold light escaping skyscrapers glass
of office blocks attended by paper ghosts
a cab pulls up alongside me still there alone
scattering thoughts at 4 AM
like neutrinos into empty space

AGNES DEI II

(..AND BLESSED SHALL BE THE MEEK...)??

Wake up you dormant spirits
Let us hear the trumpets and the horn
Heralding the new born!

A new born child came
To change the World
For now, and forever.

With Him into Millennia
We shall mark the time
For now, and forever.

Born of grief he truly was
And acquainted with pain
A man of sorrows and wisdom.

Sadly, it must be said before
Next amen Lord and Master
Your teachings do not work on Earth.

Offered forgiveness
No more cheeks to turn
Enemies hold us for fools.

IN MEMORIAM

NORMAN MCCAIG (1910-1996)

Cold January's snow sent good burghers
Scamper early to bed to rise again in the morn,
Except for you Norman McCaig the Sun set for the last time.
Scot and non-Scot alike failed to lower the flag at half-mast.
Nor did outside of Edinburgh's kirk the bells toll.
We let our best slip away quietly,
Not one or two but most and not by malice.
No fuss, no tears, no black arm band, just mired in
Slovenly non-descript materialistic indifference.

Gone with you are enigma questions directed at
The very reason for us being here in the first place.
Or why enduring honesty can only be inside of self?
Clues difficult since to trace in Cosmos disjoint,
Fallen asleep or stoned on a joyride to Hell,
Dogs-eat-dog and none is there left
Calling for your dove of peace to land.

Citizen of the world modest to a fault
You had little time for false Messiahs.
Even less for outspoken demagogues.
Misguided propaganda fools and
Certainly, least of all for dogs of war
Being the first peacenik at huge cost
Before the modern word was coined.

Calibrated and true, Norman McCaig
It would have been a privilege
To have known you in person,
Sorely McLean, Garioch, Goodsirsmith,

And McDiarmid included in the bunch.
A pleasure to share a pint with literati Scot lads,
To share a pint and your wit if not your fags.

R.I.P. Norman McCaig a bonny son of Scotland.
Son of the World, alive to this day in our hearts.
Empire comatose in 2021 sedition a dirty word.
Beautiful Highlands there back to life and free.
Launge mirk nicht of English overlord close to end:
Clouds broken blue sky's new days are shining
White cross diagonals on Du Nan Gall Highlands.

PARTING NOTE

251

At the early morning hour
Time Lord's grenadiers
in shimmering black satin come
gloved white knocking at my door
their visit card I will honor,
not on a rainy day, I hope.

If only my task was over
not left half done if at all.
To smash entry door down
there is no need,
please take a note, just
a gentle knock would do.

CACOPHONY

Landlubbers could not possibly know
How puny a fellow can be and forlorn,
Nor how endlessly long a winter night.
Until caught out by a storm Force 10
Snared by a night black as the dungeon
Single handed aboard a yacht in monster seas.
Foaming at the mouth, sea a washing machine
Poseidon's wrath unchained raging with
Sounds that you shall never forget.

Sounds of orchestra practicing cacophony
Disjoint meant to herald World Undergoing.
Sounds of groaning hull by cellos and tubas duet you hear,
In the rigging howling wind High C by first violins.
Percussions in rhythm of green one's smashing
On quarter inch of fiberglass foredeck
By Jeez, how long will she stand up to this (?),
Pummeling nonstop, only the Conductor can tell.
All this like worms nibbling at your insides.

Black as ink night closed in
Fluorescent wave tops curl and mast headlight
Glimmers of only light left in mariner's Universe,
Made to wonder how
Insignificant is, small, miniscule even microscopic the Man.
Huge and powerful beyond any measure the mighty Ocean.
Unsporting contest if ever there was one,
Battered bruised blue suffering from wet and cold.
Lone sailor cringes rolled up on the cabin floor.

Surfing down breakers stern first

Under bare poles, not a thing one can do but wait
A different kind of cold, this one gets inside the bones.
Cordage strain by sea anchor cleated to the bollard.
Opus Dei, you learn to pray and fast.
Wait for the dawn counting hours then minutes.
A year older overnight daylight break.
Almost perished for all the money.
Deserving or not in wider scheme of things
Written off sailor is forced to thank
Lady Fatima the Fate for having been spared.

*Insignificant is, small, miniscule even microscopic the Man
Huge and powerful beyond any measure the mighty Ocean.*

LOST FRIEND

Wintery nights long and bitterly cold
My old friend let it be said are
Longer and colder since you have gone.
And still, I can sense your presence
And watch image of you re-arranging furniture
In the room where once you have been.

Long walks through forest we had outside of time
Passionately discussing Psychosis of this world,
Evils on grand scale and petty point scoring
For no good purpose, it was all there no denying.
Yet I miss you my old friend; with you gone
Let it also be said there is a lot less left of mine.

Never parsimonious with words
Sharp tongues fenced for touché
As if there was still much noble
Worth spilling blood for
In the greedy perverted breed.
So here I stand my friend to have it un-said.

WHERE DID OZ HUMOR GO?

Watch our PM like a windmill industrially
In archaic locus waving arms in the air.
Four eyed Ol' Lucy in tandem right behind, and
Why am I the only one musing with a smile (?),
         While laughter one does hear
         Comes in cans all over
         The Idiot Box. Sounds from a chook pen
         Hens having laid the eggs.
Have the norms changed, has robust Oz Humor
Been irretrievably lost? Is canned laughter the best we can do?
Since innocent fun became God forbid *Strengthens verboten,*
And Big *Bro* has been watching *yu* 24/7!
         Roaming way back you would at the local Pub
         And wash down the dust with ale. Along the
         way
         Exchanging with feisty locals non-academic
         Pints of view; issue often to be duly settled
         Outside bare knuckles
         Under Lord Queensbury rules
Back inside one returned the shout and useful First Aid *info.*
And if someone called you a bastard
Short of specifically called a proper bastard
You had no reason to complain New Chum.
         2021 try to discipline out of control
         Brat screaming blue murder, no way Jose,
         Deprived   child   molester   apprehended
         in handcuffs.
         Dare cat whistle after a short hemline
         Next branded MSP to be fumigated.
Dare not pass a word that is not politically correct silly man!
No wonder we got hushed up to boring, boring, boring, boring.
For Dukes and Earls go elsewhere and we have but one Lord,

But Sir, do we have Boards and Commissions for you!
Sex, Non Discrimination, Racial Equality, Boards ad nauseum,
More boards than a timber mill and a timber shack put together.

> So, let us put to test prime suspect: eager Social Engineers!
> Black is Black and White is White still; is it not?
> Outside of Redfern anyway. Or watch your mouth *bro!*
> On about imported Goat Beards; not funny at all,
> Running all day in *nighties* head hunting the host infidel.
> So, Your Honor, who killed our humor I ask?
> High polluting Boards, precious Femme Nazis,
> Or slow heads their cousins?*Besides, yeah, Your Honor,*
> *Me name is a Peter Rabbit and I knows nuthiiin!*
> *Oh him (?), Joe Blow! He took redundancy and quit the show.*

WATERY UNDERWORLD

As I ventured into the watery underworld
Aqualungs on weaponless entering
Pristine clear waters, vanguards of the water underworld
Curious denizens advanced up to meet the intruder me.

An ocean drop off I dived into, amongst
Giant kelp grows housing sea urchins and sea stars
I saw what at first from distance looked like polka dotted
My old Mum swimming costume there with a fish tail.

With no air bubbles to be seen
As I dived closer it struck me as odd
How she managed to breathe
In this watery underworld?

Till I recognized it for what it was,
A giant potato groper out of the giant kelp
Pre-occupied shielding young fry by swimming
Side-on in front of its brood and the intruder me.

By custom I opened my empty hands towards him
Look: no weapons to do you harm my scaly friend!
To be taken by surprise as the fish swam towards me
Pictorial fins fluttering almost like in ¾ rhythm walt.

Blowing bubbles in my face from close while
Protesting in *Grouperease* guttural messages,
Possibly asking: Who in breathtaking human arrogance
Claimed all other life on Earth as mere meat and protein!

Other fishes fearlessly swam towards me large and small,
At odds with the world I knew, and so many new pals I had,
Sadly, back the next day to find a fishing trawler night before
Removed my watery underworld to city markets on dry ice.

TRAIL III

Encounters shape our life, make no mistake:
a handsome hunk met in the street
or voluptuous charming seductress
can change your compass directions, and then,

A thirteen-year-old kid goes up in smoke
and with him a wedding party of seventy.
Observed from outside bystanders look in
 "Just how sick get the morons get!"

Bathysphere bottomless deep that is
deeper still it seems is toxic Hate
stoked by bearded zealots among us
driving to impose perpetual darkness.

Just coincidence, or how else can curtains
be closing in Middle East cradle of religions
where light once shone so brightly
and prophets walked the Earth?

TRAIL IV

In search of peace
We stumble on war
When truly in love
Finding refuge from hate.

It seldom is what it seems
At first, and still, we plod on
Tirelessly on and on, till
Our faint trails only remain.